After Adlestrop

a novel by

Richard Davies

Disclaimer

This is a work of fiction. All but two of the characters in this story are fictitious.

The exceptions are the poet, Edward Thomas, whose death at the age of 39 at the battle of Arras in 1917 in World War I brought to an end a promising career as a writer and poet. He is remembered by a memorial in Poets' Corner in Westminster Abbey.

Vera Atkins was deputy head of F Section of SOE in World War 2 responsible for recruiting agents to be sent to France.

Any similarity between any other characters in the book and real people alive or dead is entirely fortuitous.

Apart from the obvious places like Oxford, London, Beaulieu, Tangmere and Poitiers, all other places like Caxton Magna and St Martin-sur-Force do not exist: they are entirely figments of my imagination.

About the author

Richard Davies is a retired diplomat who lives in Sussex with his wife and a superdog called Peggotty. He writes fiction, poetry, magazine articles and the occasional letter to The Times (some of which have even been published!)

website:www.richarddavieswrites.co.uk
contact: info@richarddavieswrites.co.uk

AFTER ADLESTROP

"I ran away from home when I was seventeen. I lived through two world wars. I was loved by and loved two wonderful men, one of whose children I bore. I was loved by and loved a wonderful woman. I have killed two men. Now, as I near the moment of my own death, I want to put down on paper what happened to me in a very long and exciting life."

My name is Mary Dumont. These are the words that my grandmother, Diana Dumont, wrote at the beginning of an account of her life. I only discovered it after my father died. I had to go out to France to clear up what had been her house and where he had lived for the last twenty years of his life. In the attic I found an old tin trunk full of things she had kept as mementoes of her life - medals I never knew she had been awarded, some bits of uniform, letters, photographs, even a small pearl-handled revolver and a box of bullets. On top of everything was a large leather bound journal in which, in her familiar round, clear hand, she had written her own story. It is a remarkable tale and one I feel I should share with anyone interested in finding out about her extraordinary life.

Inside the front cover of the book she had pasted an old newspaper cutting and a poem on which someone had written in a flamboyantly large letters: 'Dippy darling - this must have been the train you were on - much love Fizzy'. This is the article and the poem:

Edward Thomas (1878-1917) is not one of England's best known poets. Perhaps that is because he died before he could truly make his name. Young he may have been when he died, but he left a number of poems for our enjoyment and one entitled 'Adlestrop' stands out. It captures the age of steam trains, the English countryside in summer, the casualness of the unexpected and the way in which poetry can take your mind and almost throw it out into the uncharted territory of the imagination.

Thomas was travelling with his wife on the 23rd of June 1914

on his way to see the American poet Robert Frost who had rented a house near Ledbury in Gloucestershire. The poem was not published until after he died at the battle of Arras in April 1917. There is no doubt that, had he lived, he would have gone on to become one of the great English poets of the 20th Century. As it is we have a relatively small canon of work to remember him by and 'Adlestrop' will be his best known and best loved memorial. Here is his poem

Yes, I remember Adlestrop -
The name, because one afternoon
Of heat the express-train drew up there
Unwontedly. It was late June.

The steam hissed. Someone cleared his throat.
No one left and no one came
On the bare platform. What I saw
Was Adlestrop – only the name

And willows, willow-herb, and grass,
And meadowsweet, and haycocks dry,
Not whit less still and lonely fair
Than the high cloudlets in the sky.

And for that minute a blackbird sang
Close by, and round him, mistier,
Farther and farther, all the birds
Of Oxfordshire and Gloucestershire.

This is my Grandmother's story. I wish I had known all that she wrote down while she was still alive so that I could have asked her to tell me more. Despite the questions it inevitably raises and which sadly remain unanswered, it is a remarkable story and I want to share it. I have not changed one word of what she wrote:

I have been told by my doctor that I have an incurable cancer and I know that I do not have long to live. Before I die I want to put on record how I became what I am. I shall not be able to write a beautiful piece of prose. What I shall try to do instead is try to put down everything that happened to me so that my son will be able to correct my grammar and my spelling and pass this book on to my grand-daughter Mary or to anyone else whom he may think would be interested in a woman who has had by any standards an interesting life.

My name is Diana Dumont. I was born on March 10th 1897, the daughter of George Alfred Pink and his French wife, Marie Lagarde. I was christened Diana Simone after my two grandmothers. My father had been head groom at Caxton Magna, the Oxfordshire home of the Duke of Dartmoor and my mother had been personal maid to the Duchess. They left their employment when they decided to wed, it being a rule of the house that staff might not marry. Conveniently my grandfather died at about that time and they inherited the run-down livery stables in Red Lion Yard, Oxford that the old man owned. The Duke and Duchess, it seems, were sad to see their two servants go and gave them a generous wedding present of fifty guineas, which was a very large sum of money for people of their station in life in those days. With this they were able to refurbish the stables and turn the building next door into a boarding house.

My mother suffered greatly at my birth and was unable to have further babies. I therefore grew up the only child of doting parents in an environment that equipped me well for what happened to me in later life. I loved the horses and from an early age became used to handling them. My father had a gift for what he called 'talking' to them, calming them if they were frightened, schooling them patiently while speaking to them all the time. This was a skill that I inherited and, as I grew older, I was entrusted more and more with the training of ponies destined to become the first mounts for young children.

In addition to horses my father took an interest first in bicycles, which were popular with Oxford students, then motorcycles and, finally, in cars. He kept the stables going, but bought the yard next door where he could develop what he was convinced would be a growth business. So, in addition to learning all about horses, from an early age I became familiar with engines. Lord Dartmoor was the proud owner of one of the first Rolls-Royce motor cars and Father was employed to visit Caxton Magna from time to time to check that it was in good mechanical order. I used to travel out to the great house with him when he went to carry out a service and before I was twelve I knew how to look after the engine, start it up and even how to drive the car. One day, I was even allowed to take it round the stable-yard a couple of times by myself.

I went to school from the age of five and I worked hard to do well. My mother continually urged me to get a good education so that I could always keep myself if I needed to. She also taught me French because she said that it was good to know more than one language. We never went to France though. She said it was too far to travel there, but I sometimes wondered whether she did not really want to go back.

When I was sixteen I took my matriculation exams and left school. At first I helped my parents run the boarding house, the stable and the garage. After a year, though, they told me that it was time I learned a proper trade and said that they had arranged for me to go to Worcester to work in my uncle's haberdashery shop. Uncle William was not at all like his brother. He was fat, whereas my father was thin. He was loud and pompous, whilst Papa was a quiet man, who never boasted even though he had much he could have boasted about. Worst of all, Uncle William was what my girlfriends and I used to call a DOM, which stood for 'dirty old man'. Whenever he came to visit us he was forever groping at me when he had the chance. One day coming up the stairs behind me he put his hand up my skirt. I slapped his face and shouted at him that if he ever touched me again I would tell my father and he would kill him.

That seemed to stop him, but when I heard that I was to be packed off to live in his house I knew that he would take his revenge when he could. I did not dare tell my parents because I knew it would cause a terrible problem, so I went along with the plan determined that I would run away from the shop as soon as I possibly could. Where I went or what I would do after that I had no idea, but I was sure that I would be able to survive somehow.

So, on a Tuesday in late June 1914, I put on my best dress, packed a Gladstone bag with a few things to keep me going before my trunk arrived in Worcester and accompanied by Len Driver, who was my father's engineering assistant and the man everyone assumed I would settle down with one day, I went off to the station to catch the train that would carry me to what my mother called 'my new life'. Len was as assiduous as always. He was a dear man, I suppose, always kind and courteous. But he was not the man I wanted to marry and whilst I had never confided this to anyone, least of all Len himself, I knew absolutely that I would rather die than be forced to live with him for the rest of my life.

Len, who loved his pipe, found me a window seat in a 'Ladies Only' compartment, made sure that I had all I needed and went off down the train to find a Smoking carriage. I put my bag up on the rack and settled down. A few minutes later the whistle blew and the train pulled out of Oxford taking me to who knows what fate. As it gathered speed I sank into a state of black depression at the thought of my awful uncle having me in his house and my resolve to do something to escape him very soon grew the more I thought about it.

It was stiflingly hot. I tried to open the window but the fat woman next to me, who was dressed in widow's weeds and perspiring profusely, complained that she was susceptible to draughts. She then proceeded to go to sleep with her head resting on my shoulder, which grew moist with her sweat. In the seat opposite was a woman in tweeds who, when she was not coughing and then spitting copiously into a red-spotted handkerchief, kept falling asleep too, waking herself at intervals with loud snorting snores. The rest of the women packed tight into the compartment seemed so mesmerised by the movement of the train that they simply sat and stared at each other unsmilingly.

After quite a long while I felt the train slowing. This surprised me because it was meant to be a non-stop service and looking out of the window I saw that we were coming into a small station. It was obvious that it was going to stop and it suddenly occurred to me that this might be my one and only chance to escape my fate. The brakes squealed and the couplings clanked as the train came to a halt. I slid out from under the weight of my neighbour's head and stood up, took down my bag and lowered the window to look out. The platform was empty. I opened the door and stepped down, closing it as quietly as possible behind me. I looked around and saw that at the far end was a bridge and the station office. Nearer was a station sign that told me that I was at a place called Adlestrop, which I had never heard of before. I slipped behind the sign and hoped that I would be hidden from view so that no-one would see that I had left the train. Then I waited for what seemed an age but was in fact probably no more than a few minutes. The engine huffed and puffed but otherwise everything was quiet. Far down the platform a man put his head out of the window, looked around for a moment and then withdrew. In a carriage not far from where I was hiding I could see a young man sitting by an open window and gazing abstractedly into the distance. He had a long thin face, sad eyes with long lashes, large ears and a well-defined cleft in his chin. I prayed he would not shift his gaze and see me. To my great relief I heard the clunk as a signal fell and heard the engine come to life. With more clanking of the couplings and a loud hiss of steam the train got under way and in a moment it was no more than a faint noise and a plume of smoke in the distance. I moved out from behind the sign and stood for a moment wondering what on earth I was going to do.

I can still remember that moment so clearly and I suppose the young man I saw could have been the poet who wrote the poem that Fizzy sent me and which I have pasted in the front of this book. He certainly had the

7

look of a poet. If it was indeed him, then he so accurately recorded what I myself saw and heard. The air really was full of the scent of new-mown hay and there was the lovely sound of birdsong. As the noise of the train faded away all I could hear were those birds singing for what seemed like miles around. If nothing else, I recall thinking, I shall always remember this moment.

Picking up my bag I made my way to the station house expecting to find someone on duty I could speak to. I had no idea where I was nor how I was going to find my way home. But the place was locked up and I supposed that the stop the train had made was an unscheduled one and that no-one was meant to be on duty. I walked out into the station yard and then up over the bridge towards the village, the roofs of which I could see in the distance. It was very hot and the road was dusty so by the time I reached the main street I was tired and thirsty. I hoped that I might find a shop or a pub open where I could ask for a glass of water but the place was deserted apart from a tall and rather beautiful young woman with fair hair standing beside a car.

Making my way towards her I saw her suddenly kick the front wheel and shout "A curse upon the bloodstained thing!". Then she stamped her foot hard on the ground and sat down on the running board and put her head in her hands and I heard her say "Damn the stupid bloody thing. Why won't it start?"

I recognised the car as being a Rolls-Royce Silver Ghost Tourer, the latest model and a car my father had gone into raptures about when he read about it.

"Can I help you?" I asked with some hesitation.

The girl, for she could not have been much older than me, looked up, wiped her eyes with the back of her hand and scowled at me in a haughty way.

"What an earth would a village girl like you know about a motor car like this?"

She spoke so dismissively that it made me see red.

"Probably a good deal more than you think. And I'm not a village girl as you so rudely put it. I'm from Oxford and I know a lot about cars."

The girl looked at me for a long time and I thought for a moment she was going to lose her temper. Instead she burst out laughing.

"So you're from Oxford are you. The seat of all learning. All right, Miss Clever – if you show me how I can start this beastly contraption I shall for ever be in your debt. If you can't, I shall never speak to you again."

I felt really angry. Apart from her snooty manner, I disliked being rebuffed in this way.

"All right" I said "I shall see what I can manage."

Then, with my heart in my mouth because I had not the vaguest idea what I was going to do, I opened the bonnet and peered inside. The engine was mercifully quite familiar to me because of accompanying my father to Caxton Magna. I also remembered that once His Lordship was absolutely furious because his chauffeur could not start the car and Father worked out that all that was wrong was that it had run out of petrol. He showed me the knob to turn that connected the emergency fuel tank and lo and behold the car was running within seconds. Lord Dartmoor was so pleased that he rewarded my father handsomely and gave me a half a crown into the bargain.

With some trepidation I looked for the glass reservoir beneath the carburettor to see if it was full and to my relief saw that it was as dry as a bone. I then had a look inside the driver's compartment and found the knob. I turned it and went back to see what happened. Petrol was flooding into the glass and feeling very pleased with myself I told the rude girl to try to start it once more. With barely a moment's delay the engine purred into life.

The girl's reaction was completely unexpected. She put her arms around me and hugged me and kissed me.

"You really are Miss Clever and I shall love you for ever. Climb in and I shall take you to wherever you want to go."

This posed a bit of a problem for me as I did not even know where I was and certainly had no idea where I was headed. I think it was the sudden realisation of this that made me cry, for suddenly I found myself blubbing like a baby. My new 'friend for life' obviously found this most disconcerting and just stood there saying things like 'Oh my goodness' and 'What on earth is the matter?'

Eventually I managed to control myself and I told her what I had done. I do not know how I expected her to react but I certainly did not anticipate that she would burst out laughing again.

"Oh my goodness, that's wonderful and how brave of you. I don't think I would ever dare do something like that."

She could not stop laughing and clapping her hands with delight.

"You'll have to come home with me and then we can see what is to be done."

And with that she put the great car into gear and sped off out of the village along a narrow lane. My instinct was to protest but then I realised that to do so would achieve nothing. At least I was on the move and I supposed I would eventually end up somewhere that would make some sort of sense.

The car raced down narrow country lanes and through pretty villages for quite a while and then slowed as it approached two enormous pillars marking the entrance to a long drive. With a start I realised that I knew where I was – I was at the main gates of Caxton Magna. My head was already in a spin, but this made matters worse. It was like being in a sort of waking nightmare. I almost wished that I had stayed on the train, though of course, in my heart of hearts I did not. Nothing that could happen to me could be worse than having to live in the same house as awful Uncle William.

I did not say anything as we swept through the gateway and headed down the long drive to the great house at the end. Instead of going to the front, as I expected she would, she drove round to the stable-yard where I had been before. To my horror I saw that Mr Hollis, the man who had replaced my father and whom I had met each time I had been there, was standing over by the tack-room as we drove up. He came over to the car and tugged his forelock respectfully.

"There you are My Lady. I was worried because you were late back. Is everything all right?"

"Thank you Hollis. Everything is fine now, but I ran out of petrol some miles away and if it was not for this young lady I would still be there in some God-forsaken village called Adlestrop."

Mr Hollis looked mortified and then, turning to me, his face brightened.

"But you're George Pink's girl! How'd you get here, if you don't mind me asking?"

Before I could say anything my companion broke in.

"What are you talking about Hollis? Who is this George Pink?"

Then, turning to me, she asked whether I knew what he was talking about. I began to blurt out something about having been there before when Mr Hollis intervened.

"It's all very simple, My Lady. Mr Pink was my predecessor here and now runs a stables and a garage in Oxford. He comes out here from time to time to check over His Lordship's car. Sometimes Diana" he nodded in my direction "comes with him. That's how I know who she is."

"Is this true, Miss Clever?"

I felt myself blushing madly and stammered something about it being true though when I had met her I had no idea that I would end up at Caxton Magna.

"So that's how you knew what to do with the car. You are clearly a guardian angel in disguise."

She clapped her hands with glee and then turned to Mr Hollis and asked him to get the car filled up with petrol saying that she imagined she would have to drive me home before too long. Then taking me by the arm she swept me into the house, through the kitchens and out into the main part of the mansion where, of course, I had never been before. A very grand-looking butler appeared from nowhere and an order for tea and cakes was made and after he had bowed and said "Certainly, My Lady", I was then swept off into a small room at the back of the hall which was obviously somewhere my new friend treated as her own private domain.

She flung herself into an armchair on one side of the fireplace and waved me into one opposite her.

"Now – let's get everything straight, Miss Pink."

She smiled at me which reassured me somewhat, as I was by now rather frightened.

"My name is Fiona Moretonhampstead, though my best friends call me Fizzy. I know your surname but what is your other name ?"

"I'm called Diana Simone Pink." I whispered, suddenly feeling that my name sounded rather silly.

I need not have worried, for Fizzy, as I shall from now on call her, clapped her hands yet again and announced that she would henceforth call me Dippy. So Dippy I became and where she was concerned that was the end of the matter. Then she asked me to tell her my story once again and she listened attentively as I repeated what I had said about Uncle William and how when the train stopped unexpectedly I took my chance.

"But that is so wonderful." She exclaimed. "You must be a very brave person to do that. I might have done the same thing, but most girls would have just sat there and gone on to meet their grisly fate."

At that we both got the giggles and it was only the arrival of the grand butler with a tea tray that brought us back to our senses. After tea Fizzy said that I should telephone my parents to let them know that I was all right because presumably Len would have phoned them by then to tell them of my disappearance. My father was obviously relieved but angry to hear from me and it was only because I was at Caxton Magna and would be brought back to Oxford by the daughter of his former employer that enabled me to escape the worst of his wrath. Fizzy took the phone from me and I heard her tell him that she would have me back home later and that he was not to worry about a thing.

"Now" she said when she had finished her call. "What are we going to do about you. If you go back home you will be under pressure to go to Worcester as planned. If you go there you will be molested by Uncle Nasty and you will run away again. I think therefore that you should come and live here and keep me company. You are just the sort of person I have been looking for to share my life and, if you'd like to be my companion, I would be very happy to have you."

I felt the colour rising to my cheeks. The offer was amazing, though I had no idea whether I would be able to live up to her expectations. I also had no idea whether my parents would permit it. But I decided to accept in the hope that any objections could be countered and that I could start my extraordinary new life as soon as possible. Fizzy called the chauffeur and he drove us back to Oxford. She spent an hour closeted with my father while my mother fussed over me and commanded me to tell her all about Uncle William. I was certain that she was on my side and when father and Fizzy emerged from his office I could see from her face that she too had prevailed.

So it was decided that I would go to live at Caxton Magna as Lady Moretonhampstead's companion. I would be paid a small stipend and everything else would be provided for by the family. Thus, a week later, Fizzy returned and collected me, plus my trunk which had found its way back from Worcester. Mother and Father accompanied by Len Driver, who stood looking sad and a bit confused beside them, waved us off with me promising to keep in touch and to pay them visits whenever the opportunity occurred. It was the beginning of what has been a very exciting life.

Caxton Magna was a series of bewildering experiences. Fizzy herself was hard enough to keep up with, but learning to cope with her family and the army of servants was a nightmare. The Duke was kind enough to me, but either from shyness or simply because he couldn't think of anything else to say to me, whenever he encountered me about the house he always said the same thing - "Ah Miss Pink. Damned fine groom your father, damned fine." He would then stalk off intent on some unknown business.

Fizzy's mother was a rather beautiful lady who spent a good deal of her time either in London at the family house in Belgrave Square or in her bedroom – she called it her Boudoir. What she got up to in either place I cannot say and was determined to ask my mother who would doubtless know what ladies and Lady Dartmoor in particular did with their time.

Fizzy's brother, Viscount Hexworthy, who I was informed was known in the family as Hex, came and went without any apparent logic. One week he would be present at every meal and the next someone would comment that he 'must be in Paris by now' or something like that. No reason for his restless lifestyle was ever given. Indeed, I am not sure anyone really knew. He was meant to be in the Army and whenever I met him he was always talking about how we would be at war with Germany very soon, but I got the feeling that his life was dedicated to horse-racing, shooting and beautiful women. I rather liked him, but very much in the way a mouse might admire an elephant: he lived in a different universe to mine.

Fizzy's universe was something I could eventually understand because she was always busy with something and expected me to tag along and pick up the trail as I followed her. After a few days of complete panic as I tried to make head or tail of what she was up to I realised that her life revolved around her horses, her dogs and something called The Fannies which I assumed was some sort of odd club.

I shared her love of horses and one particular incident served to bond us in a way that I could never have predicted. As I have already said, Father had always been able to 'talk' to horses and make them do what he wanted. He had shown me how to do the same and one day in the stable-yard at Caxton I was able to put that art into practice and create for myself a status of my own, quite separate from that of my parents and from Fizzy, whose shadow I had become.

We had gone out to talk to the blacksmith who was paying one of his regular visits to ensure that all the horses were properly shod. I stayed talking to him – he knew my father well – while Fizzy went off to discuss something else with Mr Hollis. Some while later an almighty hullabaloo broke out in one of the loose boxes. I could hear someone screaming and a horse was neighing in a frightened way. Hollis appeared wild-eyed shouting something about Monaco, Fizzy's favourite horse, having gone mad and having pinned "her Ladyship" up against the stable wall. "He'll kill her if we don't do something!" was all he could say.

I didn't wait to be asked but ran straight to where I could hear the horse bellowing. It was just as Hollis had said. Monaco was pinning Fizzy against the wooden partition between his and the next loose-box. He wasn't hurting her as far as I could see, but was keeping her from moving and making a dreadful noise while he did so, his eyes rolling with fear. I had no real idea what I should or could do but I was convinced that this was the sort of moment where Father would have 'talked' to him and calmed him down. So I decided that I would try to do the same.

I moved very slowly towards him knowing that he could see me out of the corner of his eye and talking to him in almost a whisper as I did so. I wasn't saying anything sensible, just a jumble of words, just like Father did. As I did so I had my hand out towards him. He didn't move, which was a mercy because if he had done so he could have crushed Fizzy, but he was very wary. Something must have frightened him, perhaps a bird in the rafters or a mouse. Horses are funny creatures like that – they'll jump a huge fence without a fear, but the smallest little thing can scare them to death.

When I was near to him I blew gently at him so that he could smell my breath – Father told me that lets an animal know who it is dealing with – still talking all the while. Monaco was showing less of the whites of his eyes by then and I felt sure that he was calmer. I could hear Fizzy making sobbing noises behind him and I was still terrified that I might do something that would make the horse start and hurt her. I moved very, very slowly for the last couple of feet, talking to him all the while. Eventually I was able to put my hand out near his nostrils and I let him smell me before I tried to take hold of his halter.

Then, with my heart in my mouth, I put my fingers up behind his ears near the headband and slid them down until I could grasp the strap on his cheek beneath his eye. To my relief when I did that he lowered his head and turned towards me. I whispered to Fizzy not to move or make a noise and very, very slowly and gently I pulled the horse's head round and then began to lead him away from the side of the stall. He came with me like a baby and I led him out into the yard and walked him up and down talking to him all the while until I was certain that whatever had spooked him was forgotten. I could see Hollis and the blacksmith plus a couple of stable-lads hovering in the background. They had helped Fizzy out of the loose-box and had made to take her over to the office. But she was having nothing of that. Obviously unhurt, though doubtless shaken after what must have been a bad scare, she came over to me and when I nodded my agreement, came over and stood near to Monaco. He was completely calm by then and didn't even blink when she touched him.

Stupidly at that moment all the fear I had been bottling up overcame me and I fainted. The next thing I knew was that I was sitting in Mr Hollis's office with Fizzy kneeling beside the chair patting my hand.

The next hour or so passed in a blur. The doctor was called to attend to both Fizzy and to me. His Lordship was summoned from the Library where he liked to work. When he heard what had happened he was most solicitous towards his daughter and also to me. For the first time he did not make any mention of my Father or his qualities as a groom, but instead showed real concern that I was all right and expressed his gratitude for, as he put it, saving 'his little girl's life'.

I didn't actually save her life, of course. That said, I suppose if someone had frightened Monaco further he might have inadvertently crushed her in his panic. I didn't say so because I was so relieved that 'my trick', as Mr Hollis called it, had worked. Thereafter my relationship with Fizzy and her family, as well as with the staff in the house, changed perceptibly and I found myself being treated as a proper person in my own right rather than an appendage.

Most flattering was what Lord Hexworthy said to me next time he was at the house. He came up to me one afternoon after lunch while I was strolling by myself in the Orangery. He took my hand, pressed it to his lips and said that I would evermore have a place in his heart because I had 'saved his little sister's life'. I was so overwhelmed by his attentions that all I could do was blush and stammer something about it being the least I could have done. Then he was gone and I knew what it felt like to have been conquered by a man for the first time in my life!

Shortly after the horse thing, Fizzy told me she was going to a fanny camp and that I was to go with her. That prompted me to ask what exactly a fanny camp was. She laughed at me and called me a silly goose.

"It's the First Aid Nursing Yeomanry – I thought everyone knew that. They're known as the F-A-N-Ys for short."

I asked her what they were and she explained that it was an organisation founded a few years earlier by an Army officer who had been in South Africa during the Boer War and realised that there was a need for nurses who could ride, drive ambulances and deal with the wounded on the battlefield away from hospitals. With the prospect of war with Germany looming the FANYs were recruiting new members and were busy training. At their camps, which she said were also fun, they learned all the skills they would need when the fighting started.

So off we went to Surrey by way of the house in Belgrave Square. I had never been to London before and I was amazed at what I saw. I thought Oxford was pretty big and busy, but London was like something I could never have imagined. I found it all rather frightening, but Fizzy was completely at home there and swept me along in her usual way and made sure that I was safe and sound wherever we went. The shops and the crowds were unbelievable and I was quite glad when we drove down to Surrey after lunch on the Friday.

I had no idea what sort of place we were going to and it was only when we came to a military compound near Bisley and, having passed the guard post formalities, drove on to a circle of tents in a meadow that the reality dawned on me. I had camped with school-friends in a garden down near the river in Oxford, but had never seen anything like this. Women in khaki were everywhere, bustling in and out of a large main tent, grooming the horses tethered at the far side of the field, cooking on a smoky field kitchen and generally getting on with things. Fizzy took me into the big tent and introduced me to a lady who was obviously in charge. She didn't seem very pleased to be informed that she had a new recruit.

"Lady Fiona, surely you know the rules by now. We cannot accept just anybody into the FANYs. We have to be certain that new entrants have the right qualifications and can fit in with the rest of the girls."

Then she turned a withering eye on me and said rather fiercely.

"Well young lady, who are you and what makes you think that you could be of use to the FANYs?"

I had no idea what to say and stood there wishing the ground would open and swallow me up. Mercifully the weather interceded on my behalf. Overhead there was an enormous crack of thunder and I could hear the horses whinnying with fear. Someone outside shouted 'to the horse lines' and my interrogator closely followed by Fizzy and me ran out into the pouring rain towards where the horses were. Most of them seemed unconcerned – Fizzy told me later that they were 'battle-hardened and used to gunfire' – but one or two were obviously terrified. One was up on its back legs flailing its front hooves and no-one seemed prepared to go near it. Sensing that if I could calm it it might make the fierce lady like me more, I went towards it and began to 'talk' to it . At first it paid no attention, but slowly it seemed to calm down and lowered itself back on to four legs. It was still very nervous so it took me a while to allow me close but then, when I could do my trick of blowing up its nose it allowed me to hold its bridle and, eventually, to walk it around the paddock. By the time the other horses had calmed down I was able to take it back to the lines and tether it again.

The fierce lady came over to me.

"Well young lady, you certainly seem to be up to par on one of our requirements. What else can you do?"

"Please Madam," I said, thinking that this was no time for being a shrinking violet "I can drive and repair a motor car and I can speak French."

To my horror she burst out laughing.

"Is that so, young lady? And how are you on first aid and the sight of blood and that   sort of thing."

"I've helped people who have had accidents and I have assisted the vet when he had to operate on a horse. He said I was a good nurse."

More laughter and then to my surprise she put her arm round my shoulders and started to walk me back to her tent. Fizzy was waiting anxiously outside.

"Well My Lady" she said "It looks as though your young friend might just be the sort of person we need. She may stay and I shall decide when the weekend is over.

I think, looking back, that this was the most extraordinary experience of my life. I found myself thrust into a group of women all a bit older than me who came from the same sort of background as Fizzy and lived life in a completely different way from me. They weren't snobbish or anything like that, but they obviously soon realised that I was from a different class to them and they treated me accordingly. Had Fizzy not been there to hold my corner I would probably have run away but, as it was, by the time we left on the Monday morning I seem to have been accepted and the fierce lady told me that once my application had been properly processed I could join the FANYs.

Fizzy told me as we drove back to Caxton that she had had to be a bit what she called 'creative' with the application. I was too young it seemed and she had added a year or two to my age. She assured me that I should not worry – Fizzy was used to getting her own way in life and a little thing like my age was not going to stop her. She was right: not long after that I received a letter to tell me that I had been accepted in the Corps and Fizzy took me straight off into Oxford to order my uniform and I was soon the proud possessor of my khaki divided skirt worn over riding breeches and a khaki tunic. I remember parading around Fizzy's bedroom like a young girl in a new dress.

Fate intervened shortly after this. On the 4th of August war was declared between Britain and Germany after the Kaiser's army invaded Belgium. We first heard the news from Hex. He came dashing home to tell the family that he was off to France with what he said was to be called the British Expeditionary Force. He stayed only long enough to gather together some of his things, to kiss everyone goodbye – including me – and then to roar off in his green Crossley in a cloud of dust. I can so clearly remember Lady Dartmoor weeping as she turned back into the house comforted by His Lordship.

As they went Fizzy came over and stood beside me. She watched them enter the house and then sighed.

"Poor Mama – she was saying to me the other day that she has bad omens about this war. I pray she is wrong."

In fact she was absolutely right. Poor, dear Hex was killed at the Battle of Mons at the end of August and Her Ladyship retired to her boudoir and did not emerge from there again. She died just before Christmas. Everyone said it was of a broken heart. I did not really understand then what they meant.

But I am getting ahead of my story. The outbreak of war and then the death of her brother threw Fizzy into a frenzy of activity. She pestered the FANYs to know when she could go to France to do her bit and was furious when she heard that The War Office had rejected the Corps' offer of help. It

17

seems that they viewed it as a 'group of silly women' and had apparently written back saying that 'they did not want any petticoats here'. This was deeply disappointing for us and we had to content ourselves with raising funds and gathering equipment so that if and when the Army relented we would be ready to go.

Fizzy decided that the least she could do was to acquire a vehicle that would make a suitable ambulance and then set about converting it so that it could carry wounded men and nurses. Being Fizzy, she insisted on it being a Rolls and with my father's assistance we eventually found one that had been damaged in a collision. She instructed a coach-builder he knew to rip off the old body and replace it with something appropriate.

All this took time of course and we found ourselves with many hours to kill. I suggested to Fizzy that maybe we should start collecting things that might provide some sort of comfort for the troops as winter approached, things like socks and scarves. At first she dismissed the idea by assuring me that everybody was saying that it would all be over by Christmas but, as the weeks passed and it became clear that both sides in the war were becoming bogged down in Belgium and northern France, she agreed. With her usual enthusiasm she gathered together an enormous amount of stuff which we transported to FANY HQ - much to their consternation as there was little space for storing it all.

On one of our visits to London, wearing our uniforms because we had been to a meeting at FANY Headquarters, we were walking down The Mall when Fizzy saw an Army staff car come to a halt. A couple of young officers jumped out and then waited while a very grand-looking soldier emerged. Stiff as a ramrod, he stood and looked around him. He was about to disappear into the Admiralty Building when Fizzy let out a whoop.

"It's Uncle Bun – quick Dippy, come with me."

And we ran across the road to the car and Fizzy threw her arms round the General's neck and kissed him on both cheeks.

"Bun darling, what are you doing here?

The old man pushed her away and held her at arms length.

"Ah – Fiona. So it's you. What on earth are you doing here and in a uniform too."

"Bun, my angel – we have joined the FANYs and we are going to France with our ambulance. But the silly old War Office won't let us go. You'll do something about it for us won't you, Bun darling, you and your soldiers?"

"Fiona, my dear – my soldiers, as you call them, happen to have a very important job to do fighting the enemy and, while I am sure that what you want to do is important, you must accept that there have to be priorities."

"I know all about the war, Bun dear. I've just had my brother killed by the enemy, after all. We just want to go over there and do our bit and we find we can't."

The old man looked at her and then across at me.

"Yes – I heard about poor young Hexworthy. Tragic. I gather your Mama is quite cut up about it. Dreadful business."

Then he smiled at her and asked her to introduce me.

"This is my friend and companion Dippy – Dippy this is my lovely Godfather, General Bernard Bungay. He's the loveliest man in the world and he's going to help us get to France – aren't you Bun darling?"

"Fiona, my dear. I am but a lowly General I am afraid and I am not sure that my word will carry much weight in the War Office. But we could do with some nurses out there – it's a beastly bloodbath and our men are dying pointlessly through lack of care. I shall see what I can do, but no promises."

He smiled at us .

"Now my dears, I have a meeting to go to and must hurry."

He saluted me and shook my hand, kissed Fizzy, murmured more condolences for her brother and marched off into the building. I stood there speechless. I still couldn't understand how Fizzy's world worked. She seemed to know everyone and had no fear in using her connections whenever she needed something. It was all so different from the world I knew.

"He's a darling man and I am sure he'll pull some strings." She said, then took my arm and marched me off down The Mall towards Buckingham Palace.

Sad to relate nothing came of whatever General Bungay did or said, if of course he did actually do anything, and Christmas came and went with still no word from the FANYs.

The death of Fizzy's mother cast a dark pall over us all and her father, who had taken the loss of his son and then his wife terribly badly, became a sad shadow of his former self. After the funeral, which was combined with a memorial service for Hex whose body had been interred in a field somewhere in Flanders, he took to spending even more hours alone in the Library just sitting in a chair staring out of the window or dozing. One day I had to go in there and, though I was as quiet as I could be, he woke as I was on my way out.

"Ah, Miss Pink."

He held out his hand to indicate that I should go over to him.

"To what do I owe the pleasure of this visit to my hiding place?"

I told him that I had come to fetch a magazine that Fizzy wanted.

"Do you enjoy being with us? It's not a very happy household these days, I fear."

"I'm very happy, My Lord. I am only sorry that such sadness has come to you. I wish there was something I could do to help."

"There is, my dear, there is. I want you to promise me that you will keep Fiona safe. She is a headstrong girl, like her mother was when I married her. And I know that she is capable of doing things that can put her life at risk. If you are determined to go off to the war, I beg you to make sure that she does not put herself and of course you in any more danger than is necessary. Will you do that for me, my dear?"

Then he struggled to his feet and went over to his desk, pulled open a drawer and took a small package from it. He brought it back to where I had stayed standing.

" Take this and keep it safe. It is only for use if you feel it is really necessary."

He handed over the parcel and told me to open it. Inside was a leather case containing a small pearl-handled revolver and a box of bullets. I had never seen a gun before and I must have gasped.

"Do not be frightened, my dear. It is not dangerous, except of course if you put bullets in it, point it at someone and pull the trigger. It is only for use if you and Fiona are in real danger. Once this beastly war is over I hope you will return it to me never having been fired."

I took the gun, put it back in its case and left. I was terrified and went immediately to put it amongst my clothes in the room I slept in next to Fizzy's. I resolved never to use the thing, though fate had other plans, as I would one day find out.

The call for us to go to join the FANYs in France came in January 1915. An earlier contingent had gone out just as the first battle of Ypres was raging and had established themselves in an old school near the Cathedral in Calais.

It was a strange moment for me. I had taken a difficult farewell of my parents. My mother had talked to me since I was a little girl about growing up on the outskirts of Paris and she had ensured that I spoke some French and now she was excited that for the first time I was going to see it for myself. She had pressed upon me a list of addresses of relatives should I find myself near where they lived. My father reminded her that I was going to the war zone and that it could be dangerous and this tempered her enthusiasm. Fizzy had come with me to see them and she assured them that she would take care of me. I had to smile to myself because I knew that I would be saying the same to her father when we said goodbye to him the next day.

Poor old Lord Dartmoor was tearful when he waved us off. I think he genuinely feared that we would not return and that not only would he be alone but that the long lineage of the family would come to an end. There was no heir and the only hope lay in Fizzy marrying and having a son. He looked somehow older and smaller as he waved us off, surrounded by the staff at Caxton Magna. Fizzy drove at speed down the drive and out onto the road to London. Only when we were some miles away did she stop and put her head in her hands.

"Oh Dippy – I'm so frightened. I know I pretend to fear nothing, but I don't want to die and I have a horrid feeling that I am going to."

I said nothing – what could I say. I just hugged her and waited for her recover her composure and press on.

We drove the ambulance which Fizzy had christened Boanerges – she told me it meant Son of Thunder, but I could not see the connection – down to Dover and having helped some of the wounded who had been repatriated and who were lying helplessly on stretchers on the dockside in the rain, we eventually managed to embark on a ferry and crossed the channel in a howling gale.

Calais was like a scene from Hell in one of those old religious pictures. Thousands of people were milling about amid the horses and carts and the trains. Some were soldiers on their way up to the front, others were wounded men on their way home. Then there were refugees fleeing the Germans and the battlefields looking desperate, clutching bundles of possessions yet with nowhere to go.

With difficulty we found Lamark, the school where the FANYs were based. For a while I had feared we would have to spend the night in Boanerges. Luckily my faltering French was enough to make a policeman understand and he jumped on the running board and guided us to it.

The sight that met our eyes was not one to inspire confidence. It was a ramshackle place which smelled of drains and garlic and it was basic in the extreme, despite the efforts of the girls who had been there for a while. There were wards for the wounded and others for civilian typhoid victims, though they were on the ground floor away from the soldiers. The sanitation was basic.

Almost immediately we got there a Zeppelin flew over and dropped bombs on the town. Mercifully none came near us that day, though not long afterwards there was a direct hit on the cathedral which blew out all the windows in the hospital. To accustom ourselves to the place we were tasked for the first week or two to drive out towards the front distributing what they called 'comforts' to the troops – clean socks and shirts and so forth.

One time, later on in May, we had to go with the mobile kitchen which meant that we were close to the front for nearly a week, sleeping under the vehicle and having to boil soup on a very inadequate stove for hungry and frightened men. The front was a terrifying place to visit. Yet another vision of hell. Oceans of mud, the stink of death everywhere – human bodies were buried whenever possible but horses were often left to rot or to be eaten by stray dogs and rats. We were issued with masks for that trip because there had been tear-gas attacks against the French lines and men were coming back from the front line badly affected.

Looking back, I'm not quite sure how Fizzy and I survived. After the comforts of Caxton Magna the shock to the system was immense. I think, on reflection, it was only the fact that all the other girls were in the same boat that made it bearable. It was almost impossible to have a bath and washing clothes was a nightmare, not least because there was always the risk that anything hung out to dry would be stolen. Our companions were a most remarkable band of women. Despite the constant barracking from the soldiers and the cavalier way we continued to be treated by the Army High Command we stuck at it regardless. We were there to serve the Belgian Army of course, for it was not until the end of 1915 that agreement was reached for us to be part of the British effort. We were teamed up with the Red Cross Society and the Order of St John even though we had worked with British wounded from the start whenever the need arose.

The work was incredibly hard, so much so that I sometimes woke in the morning and almost prayed for a bomb or a shell to fall on me and put me out of my misery. But we survived, grabbing any chance for leave that presented itself. We went to Paris once and I searched for my Mother's relatives, but found no-one who knew of her. It was, after all, more than twenty years since she left home and she had not been a good correspondent, so perhaps that was not a surprise. We also went back to England a few times, driving wounded men who needed special care on the journey rather than having to face the hazards of travelling back on a troopship. Caxton Magna had been turned into a convalescent home for the wounded and Fizzy's father had moved into one of the keeper's cottages on the estate.

The biggest impact of the war on my home was that though my father was too old to be called up he was commandeered by the Oxfordshire Regiment and made use of whenever they had problems with either their horses or their vehicles and was much in demand. My mother ran the stables and the boarding house single-handed and the mechanical side was left to Len

Driver until he was called up and went off to fight.

Sadly, poor Len did not make it. He was killed right at the end of the war, on the day before the Armistice was signed which always seemed to me to be such a tragic irony. He was a dull man but he deserved better.

Fizzy and I remained close throughout our time in France. We needed each other to maintain our morale and our relationship changed from that of an aristocratic lady and her companion to that of close personal friends. Amazingly, given what seemed so important to many of the people I came across at this time, the class thing did not seem to matter to her. We were chalk and cheese but never once did she ever suggest that I did not 'know my place' as they say. We became and remained until she died the closest of friends. We shared many moments of danger, but only once did I have to follow her father's instructions and use the little pistol when I thought she was likely to come to real harm.

That moment came in late 1917 when we had been moved to an old Cistercian monastery on the River Marne at Port à Binson. Shortly after we arrived there Fizzy had hurt her arm swinging the starting handle on a lorry and was 'confined to barracks' until she recovered. This meant that she was expected to do things like fold bandages and check medical stores. I was usually out driving the ambulance and caring for those I brought in from the front. I had taken to carrying the pistol, which I kept loaded in case it was ever needed, almost from the beginning because I did not want to leave it with my other things. There had been a fair amount of stealing in Calais and it became a habit to carry anything valuable on one's person. Not that we had much worth taking after more than two years in the heart of the battle.

Anyway, one day I returned with my 'passengers' and then went in search of Fizzy. As I neared the bandage room where she was working that day I heard her voice raised in anger and then a scream. I rushed to open the door and saw to my horror that she was on the bed with her skirt torn and a man with his trousers down was trying to rape her. She was beside herself with fear and not thinking I took the little gun from my pocket and shouted at the man to stop. I think he was drunk – this happened sometimes when soldiers found a wine cellar in a bombed out building - for he turned to look at me without letting go of Fizzy's throat and told me very rudely to go away. I raised the gun and told him that I would kill him if he did not release her.

He laughed and told me to go ahead. He said he would rather die between a woman's legs than in a trench. So I shot him in the leg. The noise was enormous and I was terrified by that more than his reaction. He screamed with pain, threw Fizzy off the bed and lunged at me in a fearsome rage. He tripped and fell because his trousers were round his knees, but this did not prevent him from grabbing at my skirt and hauling himself up onto his feet. I could smell the alcohol on his breath and see the anger in his eyes. He shouted that he would deal with me once he had finished with Fizzy and turned to grab her again. She screamed loudly so I shot him again.

He turned to face me and then fell dead at my feet, blood seeping from the wound in his chest where the second bullet had gone. Fizzy was still sitting whimpering on the bed, too shocked to speak. I went over to her to make sure she was all right. She had a black eye and scratch marks on her neck but I could see that she was otherwise unhurt. I asked her if he had actually managed to do to her what he intended and she shook her head.

I then turned to look at the man. He was in a uniform I did not recognise. He wore no signs of rank so I assumed he was a private soldier. Perhaps a Canadian or an Australian: I did not know. My only concern was to be rid of him as quickly as possible. It shocks me now to recall it, but I remember thinking like a criminal wishing to dispose of the evidence. I was not worried about the fact that he was dead – I saw dead men by the score every day of my life at that time. It was rather that I did not want to have to tell anyone about what had happened and, in case someone had heard the screams and then the shots, I wanted to get rid of him as quickly as possible.

I told Fizzy to stay where she was and I ran to fetch Boanerges. Then together we put the body on a stretcher and took him to the ambulance. I left Fizzy there and drove to the French Army mortuary down the road and with a calmness that I did not know I possessed I informed the men in charge that I had been asked to bring the body to them and left them to carry it away to be buried. I don't think they gave him a second look. They were so used to bodies that they no longer bothered, especially if it was not one of theirs. I then drove back to the monastery, found Fizzy and devoted my energies to making sure that she had recovered from the experience.

Her ordeal had not hurt her physically, but she was shocked by both the ferocity of the attack and the invasion of her privacy that it threatened. I realised that she was completely unused to a world in which men behaved with animal passion when drunk or otherwise aroused. For all her strength of personality and courage I could see that she was very vulnerable when unfamiliar things happened to her. I had to take her in hand and tell her what to do.

"Fizzy we cannot report this. No-one should know that you were attacked and certainly not that I killed the man. Do you understand."

She nodded and cried some more. Then it was my turn to go to pieces. The enormity of what I had done came home to me and now it was she who had to do the comforting as I sobbed on her shoulder. The truth was that I was terrified that someone would find out and I would be punished. This was a fear that stayed with me for the rest of the war and, indeed, still concerns me all these years after. It doesn't matter now – I am going to die and I have said my prayers and confessed to God, asking him to understand that I was saving a life by taking one. I pray He will understand.

Fizzy recovered from the attack within a day or two and, as by then her arm was also much better, we returned to our duties with the ambulance and tried to forget the whole thing. That was not too difficult as we had so much to do. The scale of the slaughter at the front did not diminish and the roar of the cannons which caused so much death and destruction was constantly in the background as we worked. Only when the Battle of Passchendaele was over could we relax a bit.

Then without warning in 1918 we were moved back to Calais as the French had decided to take over our hospital at Port à Binson. There we were frequently bombed by Zeppelins and shelled from the sea by German warships. The wounded came in droves and then, after another move to St Omer, the front was getting closer as the Germans tried to force their way south. On two occasions we were told that we would have to leave, possibly to go back to England, but in the end the Allied armies were able to break out of the stalemate that trench war forced on them and I suppose you could say that that was when the end of the war began.

Peace came in November and Fizzy and I found ourselves rather left to our own devices. We planned to drive home in Boanerges, which despite the rigours of three years in the most terrible conditions, had survived pretty much intact. But that was not to be.

One day shortly after the Armistice was signed we were driving along and witnessed the crash of a French Army bi-plane. We drove to the spot to see if we could help. The pilot was dead but the observer in the rear seat, a junior army officer, had survived the impact with just a broken leg. My French had improved after three years, but even so my accent must still have sounded funny because he laughed when I told him that we could take him to a hospital. Despite the pain he must have been in, he had a beautiful smile and I think it was that that attracted me to him first of all.

We took him to a nearby first aid station where his leg was put in plaster and then we carried him back out to the ambulance. He then asked if we could drive him to Paris where he had relatives This we agreed to do and I had no thought then that I would ever see him again when we had done so. But jokingly Fizzy told him that we would be happy to drive him all the way to his home if he wanted and he said that if we were willing to go as far as Aquitaine then he would be happy to pay for the petrol and to reward us for our efforts. My instinct was to refuse his offer, mainly because I was uncertain what he was up to, but Fizzy jumped at the chance and so, after she had hastily written a letter to her Father to explain that our return home would be delayed, we set off.

Jean-Paul Dumont was the most beautiful man I had ever come across. He had none of the swagger of poor dead Hex and none of the authority of so many of the military men I had had to deal with, but to me he had elegance, charm and, above all, the ability to make me laugh. The attraction I had felt right from the beginning turned into love as I got to know him better – I wanted him like I have never wanted anything else in my life. When I told Fizzy this she looked sad. I was hurt, but I put it down to jealousy.

Jean-Paul lived in a place called St Martin-sur-Force in the Dordogne - the very village where I am writing this journal more than seventy years later. It took us nearly a week to get there. The roads were bad at first and even when they improved as we got further from the battlefields we had to drive slowly and stop frequently because of our patient. It was nearly Christmas by the time we reached his home and we were thankful for the goatskin coats that had become a sort of FANY uniform over the winters of the war, great hairy things that had become something that contributed to the controversial status of the Corps.

Jean-Paul's condition had been complicated during our journey by the fact that he developed some sort of fever, which neither of us were really qualified to treat. We resorted to giving him aspirin, which we had in the ambulance and to sponging him down regularly. This worked, much to our relief, and we reached his home with him in reasonable condition. It came as an enormous relief to take the lane that wound down the river valley to the village nestling in a hollow below and to deliver him to his family..

He lived with his parents in a rather grand village house. His father, he had explained, was the leading citizen of the village and owner of much of the enterprise in the surrounding district. Jean-Paul explained to us the night before we arrived that Monsieur Dumont was a farmer, not a bourgeois who had inherited his wealth. He had become rich by dint of hard work and good judgement, what I suppose you would call a yeoman in England.

The family knew nothing of our imminent arrival and an ambulance turning up in the courtyard of their house at dusk on a cold December day caused a real furore. His mother was hysterical to see him in such a conveyance and could only be calmed down by me explaining in my faltering French that all that was wrong was a broken leg and that they were very lucky that he had survived the plane crash. Jean-Paul's father huffed and puffed in the background and then summoned some of his farm-hands from their lodgings on the edge of the village to come and carry the young man into the house.

We were rather left to our own devices then and it was only when Jean-Paul told his mother that we had brought him home out of kindness that she came to us and fussed over us like a mother hen. She was terribly impressed that Fizzy was a Countess (I had to use the French word 'Comtesse' as I could think of no other way to describe her) which amused me as I had always thought the French had taken great pleasure in beheading all their aristocrats in their revolution. We were treated with great kindness and hospitality and they insisted that we stay for a few days to recover from our journey.

It was during this time that I found out that my love for Jean-Paul was reciprocated. Someone had found an old bath-chair and I used to push him around the garden and through the village when the weather permitted. I had found early on in our journey down that he spoke some English and this combined with my basic French meant that we were able to communicate reasonably well. We got to know each other better and better. On one of our circuits of the village square when, as usual, we were followed by a horde of giggling children, he told me that he thought I was the nicest and most beautiful girl he had ever met and he asked me whether I would like to marry him. I was flabbergasted by this and did not know what to say. I just told him that I would have to think about it and to show that I meant it I kissed him on the cheek.

Back at the house I found Fizzy and took her into garden to tell her what had happened. Once again she looked sad when I told her that I was inclined to accept his offer. I had added that of course I would not dream of deserting her if she felt she needed me, but after more than four years together and after all we had been through I somehow felt that the time had come for me to move on and make a life for myself.

"Oh Dippy – I thought this might happen."

I saw that there were tears in her eyes.

"I have feared this moment ever since you told me how you felt about him. I know you must do what is best for you, but I shall miss you so much if you leave me. You have saved my life twice and I fear that without you I shall be defenceless and vulnerable."

I felt terrible. Part of me did not want to leave her – so much had happened to me since that day in Adlestrop. But deep inside me I ached more than ever with love, or desire, or whatever it was, for Jean-Paul.

I gave Fizzy a hug and she wrapped me in her arms and kissed me on the neck and just held me tight for ages. Then she stood back.

"You must come back to England with me first, Dippy. I insist. I can't just go back alone. I shall need you there."

So it was arranged. I told Jean-Paul that I loved him and would return in the Spring so that we could wed. We agreed that we should be married at Easter and that I would come back as soon as I could so that we could prepare for our life together. We stored Boanerges in one of Monsieur Dumont's barns and, having said our farewells, travelled back to London by train. I felt ecstatic and yet I couldn't shake off the feeling of guilt Fizzy had instilled in me. It was only when we found ourselves back in London that I began to feel stronger in my resolve both to marry Jean-Paul and to resist the none too subtle pressure Fizzy was putting on me. It was her father who won the day for me in the end.

We found him at the house in Belgrave Square, where he had retreated as Caxton Magna started to overflow with convalescent soldiers and the keeper's cottage proved inconveniently small for someone used to more space. He looked much older and was pathetically pleased to see his daughter again. His welcome to me was generous too and he referred to Fizzy and me more than once as 'his two girls'. I did not have a chance to talk to him alone during the first two days there, but after breakfast on the third while Fizzy had dashed out to see a friend who lived nearby, he took me into his study, sat me down in a large leather armchair next to his desk and asked me to tell him what we had been up to.

"There's no use asking Fiona. She never gives me a straight answer to anything I ask her. Never has – just like her dear mother."

He looked away for a moment, staring into the distance.

I told him everything from the beginning. I did not mention the man who had tried to rape Fizzy nor that I had used the gun, but when I had finished my account of our years in France he asked me directly.

"Thank you, Miss Pink. No - I shall call you Diana now - you're quite part of the family after all. You have had a rare adventure, both of you and thank the Good Lord you have returned safely. I could not have borne it if I had lost both my children and my wife."

He looked away again. Then he blew his nose loudly and turned back to me.

" And that little pistol – did you ever have need of it?"

My instinct was to say nothing, but somehow I felt I should, so in the end I poured the whole story out.

"By Jove, Diana, You've got some courage. Thank you my dear.

Thank you for saving my daughter from what was likely to have been a dreadful experience, if not worse. I don't know how to show you my gratitude, but I shall think of something, you mark my words."

He smiled and patted me on the knee.

"And what now, my dear? Have you and Fizzy hatched some great plan while waging war against the Kaiser?"

I told him about Jean-Paul and my decision to go back to France to marry him.

"You are sure about him, Diana? Is this possibly a rash decision upon which you should reflect?"

"Oh no, My Lord. I know that I love him and I know that I will marry him. My only concern is for Fizzy - Fiona – who seems very upset by my decision. The last thing I want to do is to upset her, but I feel that if I say no to Jean-Paul I shall regret it for the rest of my life."

"Then, Diana, you must follow your heart. You have my blessing for what it is worth. What do your parents say?"

I explained that I had yet to see them and he insisted that I let his chauffeur drive me to Oxford to tell them that I was safe and of my plans. At that moment Fizzy returned and insisted on coming with me, so we set off together in Lord Dartmoor's very grand car to see my mother and father.

It was strange going back to Red Lion Yard. I had seen so much of the world since the day Fizzy had driven me off to my new life. We were greeted with wild enthusiasm and were made to sit down and tell them all about our adventures. Afterwards they broke the news to me that Len Driver had died and that rather put a dampener on what until then had been a jolly occasion.

My mother looked older and tired and later while he was showing me around the yard my father said that she had been unwell - 'something wrong with her insides' was how he put it – but would not go to see a doctor. I told him I would ensure that she did so and in the end Fizzy and I managed to persuade her that it was the best idea to seek an expert's opinion and an appointment had been made with a specialist at the Radcliffe Infirmary for the very next day. It was not the first time that I had watched the magic of the Dartmoor family name open doors that would have been closed to anyone else. In addition to fixing the date she also told the Doctor that the account for the consultation and any subsequent treatment should be sent to her.

My father looked much the same, though perhaps a little greyer at the temples and a little slower in his movements. He and Fizzy got on like a house on fire and I enjoyed sitting back and watching them chat away together, very aware of the way in which my life had changed since I was last there.

The news of my impending marriage was received with some concern which focused mainly on the impossibility of them being there for the occasion. Fizzy dismissed their concerns and told them that she would ensure that they were transported there and back even if she had to drive them herself. I was then able to extol Jean-Paul's virtues to them and to reassure them that I would be marrying well.

The day finished with me walking round to Mrs Driver's house down by the canal to offer my commiserations. She was inconsolable and it brought home to me that all over the country there must be homes like hers that were overlaid with grief at the loss of fathers, sons and husbands, so many of whom we had nursed and, regrettably, dispatched to the mortuary. What a dreadful war it had been. The loss of life had been terrible, not just for us, but for the French and, I had to admit, the Germans too. It still makes me shudder as I write this so many years later.

Fizzy and I spent the night at Caxton Magna and it gave us both great pleasure to wander through the place and out into the grounds in the peace and quiet of the countryside. We had each been marked by the noise and brutality of the war, though I suspect at the time neither of us would have admitted as much. But it was also a sad place to be, now that Lady Dartmoor was dead and poor, dear Hex lay in a grave near Mons. The staff numbers had been considerably reduced and the park and the gardens near the house looked neglected.

"I wonder if Daddy will ever come back here." Fizzy mused.

"Of course he will and so will you."

"Oh Dippy dear, I don't think so. I won't anyway, that's certain and I think that poor darling Daddy has a broken heart too and will one day just curl up and die. I'm all he's got left, you know and he so wanted poor Hex to inherit the title and carry on the line."

"But you could do that. Marry someone and have a son. That would solve the problem."

There was a long silence and then Fizzy said something that rather shocked me.

"I don't want to marry, Dippy. I don't think I like men very much. I'd like to marry you, but that's not allowed."

Then she laughed and turned away, but not before that I could see that there were tears in her eyes. At the time I did not understand what she was talking about and I felt it was probably better to leave things like that.

The doctor at The Radcliffe examined my mother the next day and announced that she needed an urgent operation. It was arranged that this should happen immediately to leave enough time for convalescence before my wedding. Fizzy assured her that she would look after all the arrangements and mother told me later that she was very relieved to know that something was going to be done. She had not gone to see a doctor because she feared that she had some sort of tumour and was going to die. But if the doctor was correct and she would feel much better after the operation, then she was happy to have it. I told my father the news and he also showed obvious relief. I think he, too, had feared the worst.

Fizzy and I went back to London that evening and I began to prepare for my return to St Martin and for my wedding day. We shopped for my trousseau at grand stores the like of which I had never seen in my life, places on Oxford Street like Marshal & Snelgrove and Mr Selfridge's grand emporium. Fizzy very sensibly said that as I was going to live in the country and be a working wife I would need clothes that were appropriate. She also insisted that I would need some things that were more sophisticated so that when Jean-Paul wanted to 'show me off' he could be proud of his English bride. I therefore acquired a wardrobe of garments that made me feel like a princess and Fizzy insisted on paying for everything. This embarrassed me and also made me angry because I felt she was treating me a bit like someone who needed her charity. In a way that was true of course - I had hardly any money nor did my parents, certainly nowhere near enough to make the shops she chose affordable. I said this to her and to my surprise she was quite upset. She explained that she wanted to do it for me both as a wedding present and because she loved me dearly and wanted to show it. I did not know how to respond: indeed, I did not know exactly what she meant and the intensity of what she said and how she said it puzzled me. I knew she was hurt, but I did not know why and thought it best to do and say nothing more on the subject.

It all blew over, of course, and our friendship was as close as always, but in the back of my mind was the thought that Fizzy was perhaps jealous of me finding someone to love and to marry. Nothing further was ever said and as the weeks passed and it came time for me to return to France to prepare for the wedding we were as close as we had been during the war years. I had stayed in Oxford while my mother had her operation and then nursed her back to health. By the time she had recovered enough to travel it was late March and I knew I had to ready myself for the big day.

Easter Day 1919 fell on 20 April and I had promised to be back in St Martin at least a week before that. My parents proposed that we travel together. We went first to Paris where I met the relatives I was supposed to have visited during the war. We spent the good part of a week there seeing the sights and being introduced to family members that even mother did not know. It was fun but exhausting and I was relieved when we set off again to travel south. We took an express to Limoges and then a local train to Thiviers where Jean-Paul and his father met us. The last stage of the journey was in a horse-drawn coach followed by a cart with all our luggage.

The Dumont family made us very welcome at their home at St Martin and even though my mother found it took her some time to get to know Jean-Paul's mother, our respective fathers shared a number of interests and although they could not really communicate with each other they spent many happy hours together in the stables and barns surrounding the house.

A little later Fizzy drove down in her new two-seater Rolls, a beautiful yellow machine with black wheels. She arrived in the village on Good Friday, April the 18th as only she could, with a roar and a squeal of brakes as she came to a halt outside the house creating a cloud of dust, scattering chickens far and wide, frightening the horses and bringing the whole population to their windows to see what had broken the normal peace and quiet of the place. Even though the Dumont family had met her before, they still found it hard to adapt to the presence of a flamboyant 'milady' in their midst. I know Fizzy tried her best to fit in with them all, but try as she would she could not help but put her foot in it at every turn. There was an almost audible sigh of relief when she left to stay in the hotel in Périgueux that she had booked from London.

The wedding was a splendid affair even though poor Jean-Paul was still unable to walk properly as he did not have the plaster-cast removed from his leg until a week before the ceremony. The break had healed but his muscles had wasted and he found walking difficult at first. He was pushed down the aisle in his bath-chair and then helped to stand beside me supported by crutches.

We made our vows, said our prayers, took communion and then were whisked off to the Mayor's office – ironically Monsieur Dumont was the current mayor – for the civil ceremony and that meant that at last we were properly married. My love for Jean-Paul was as strong as ever it had been and it was the most beautiful and happy day of my life. Even Fizzy seemed happy for me.

We went away on our honeymoon in a carriage drawn by four white horses, swept off to spend the first night in Périgueux and then to take the train to Bordeaux and on to the seaside at Arcachon. Our first week together was bliss – I can still remember how happy I was more than seventy years later.

The happiness lasted for three more years. I became pregnant almost immediately and early in 1920 I gave birth to twins – a boy called

Charles after Jean-Paul's father and a girl we christened Marie after my mother. By then Jean-Paul's leg was completely better though he still walked with a slight limp. As we used to say to each other he was lucky to be alive – a limp was a small price to pay.

As a wedding present Monsieur Dumont had given Jean-Paul the brick and tile works he owned up on the main road. There was a large house behind it and we made our home there. The factory was run down because most of the men who once worked there had been taken off to fight in the war and so many of them died in the trenches. We recruited new workers and rebuilt the business. I decided that in addition we should use the lorries and carts that transported the bricks and tiles to do general haulage as well. I also set about turning the forecourt of the works into a garage where passing motorists could buy petrol and where we could offer mechanical services and sell cars. People laughed at me and said it would never work, but we quickly found that it was a success. The transport side grew too and we added a bus service to local towns and had a charabanc that we hired out. The future looked good. We were working hard but we were making money. The children flourished and life was as perfect as it could be.

Then just before Christmas in 1923 fate intervened and changed my life once again, but this time in a dreadful and cruel way. One morning the men were loading a consignment of tiles onto a lorry when something slipped and they all fell on top of Jean-Paul. That did not kill him, but by the time the doctor came he had lost a lot of blood and his pulse was very weak. I had sent one of the men to fetch Boanerges from the barn in the village and when he returned with the old ambulance we put him inside just as Fizzy and I had done when we rescued him from the crashed plane. Then we set off towards Nontron where there was a small clinic. I was seized with a terrible sense that I was somehow reliving the past. This time, though, my efforts were in vain. He died on the way, his head cradled in my arms and his face wet from the tears that I could not stop shedding. He had never regained consciousness and I regret even to this day that I was unable to say goodbye and to tell him how much I loved him.

After Jean-Paul's death my life became a sort of living hell. Apart from my grief and the uncertainty of my future and that of the twins, his family seemed to turn against me. I know that, though they had welcomed me into the family, I had always been distrusted because I was in their eyes a foreigner despite my French mother. Now they seemed to want to blame me for what happened to him, which was so unfair and hurtful. I felt unloved and almost in danger. At his funeral there was a lot of muttering and sideways glances in the church and also at the graveside and though my grief must have been obvious, few came to commiserate with any apparent sincerity. I was not surprised – St Martin was a very closed community, suspicious of the outside world and especially of foreigners, a word that encompassed residents of neighbouring towns and villages as well as non-French people like me – but it was nevertheless terribly hurtful at a time when I was desperate for someone on whose shoulder I could lean. They were dark days.

I had written to Fizzy to tell her all about my plight as soon as the accident happened and had asked her to come to see me when she could. She did not reply and I resigned myself to the fact that she was probably away from home and had not received my letter. Then to my astonishment she turned up in the village a week later on a motorcycle, a brand new and rather noisy Velocette especially adapted to be ridden by a woman. She had put it on the train to Paris, ridden it across the city to catch a train to Thiviers and then raced on it through the Dordogne countryside to be with me. Despite my overwhelming sadness, I had to laugh as she peeled off her flying helmet and goggles in the square at St Martin: yet again she had managed to completely confound me as well as the whole village who had gathered to stare at her.

It was a huge comfort to have Fizzy there and I felt better able to deal with Monsieur and Madame Dumont with her at my side. Indeed, their instinctive respect for 'their betters' - the sort of thing they would of course claim had died out, literally, in the Revolution- showed through the moment 'Milady' appeared on the scene again. She not only convinced them that Jean-Paul's death was a tragic accident, but turned them from grieving and accusing opponents into loving and helpful parents-in-law again who understood not only my own personal grief but my huge sympathy for them too. Bit by bit I managed to re-assemble my life. Caring for the children helped and having Fizzy there to talk to worked magic.

They were still dark days, but then three things happened that changed my life in all manner of ways and, I have to say, as well as making it happier they also made it rather complicated.

I had decided to sell the brickworks, because I could not bear to be associated with an enterprise that had taken my beloved Jean-Paul away from me. I also decided to close down the garage and moved the transport business I had developed to the other side of the village. That meant that I had to give up the house behind the works and in any case I could not bear to live and bring up my children where he had been so gravely injured.

So I began to look for somewhere to live. I did not want to take the house kindly offered by Monsieur and Madame Dumont, not because I did not appreciate their offer, but because I wished to establish my own identity and declare my independence of the family. As you can probably imagine, this did not go down too well and it was due to Fizzy's diplomatic intervention that they came to understand.

My search at first was fruitless. There was not much that I could hope to buy and what there was did not appeal. There were many properties standing empty but that was usually due to some complex family quarrel over a will and they were not for sale. In the end it was through some obscure connection of Fizzy's with family of the Marquis de St Martin, whose family had owned the whole district before the Revolution, that offered the ideal solution. Fizzy had stayed a few days in Paris on her way back from a visit to London to see her father. There she had been introduced to a member of the St Martin family who, she said, was obviously down on his luck. On hearing where she was bound, he told her that he had a house called La Garenne near the village that he would like to sell and offered it to her for an attractive price. She declined the offer, but said that she knew someone who might well buy it. He suggested that she contact his lawyers in Périgueux so that I could inspect the house.

Fizzy and I went to have a look and I fell in love with it immediately. Although I had come to know the village and its environs quite well in the years I had lived there, for some reason I had never been on the land that still belonged to the Marquis' family. As soon as I saw the old building I was captivated, even though it was in a terrible state and needed a huge amount doing to it. Fizzy and I explored like a couple of children and by the time we had finished I had no doubts that it was where I wanted to live.

The Notaire, who showed us around, told us that the house had been built using the stones and timbers from the château that had been on the site and which had been virtually demolished in the Revolution. In consequence there were many rather grand features that reminded me a little of Caxton Magna. Fizzy, of course, could not see any similarity at all, but she loved the place as much as I did and encouraged me to buy it even though, when the moment came, I had dreadful cold feet. It brought home to me that fact that I was now on my own in what was still a strange country. Jean-Paul had been so supportive – I would have to cope by myself.

Fizzy's enthusiasm helped me to overcome these doubts and fears and the upshot was that within a few weeks I became the proud owner of La Garenne and this rambling old house has been my home ever since. Before I could move in there was a huge amount to be done. Not least, because it had been virtually uninhabited for decades, there was a mass of rubbish and clutter to be moved out of the place. An old man, not quite a vagrant but someone who had opted out of village life years before had lived in one of the rooms and he had a left a dreadful and insanitary mess.

We systematically cleared the place out, threw   anything that could be burned on a huge bonfire that seems in retrospect to have burned for weeks and we used one of my lorries to transport anything that could not be burned to a scrapyard near Nontron. It was filthy, disgusting work yet the process of revealing the rather beautiful features of the house that had remained hidden for so long was enormously exciting and I grew to love the place more and more as we scrubbed, swept and dusted. The transformation was immediate and amazing. Then the carpenters, plumbers, electricians and stonemasons moved in and did all the work that I had decided was needed to turn it into the sort of home I wanted for my children. The whole village helped me move and Fizzy stayed on for the rest of the summer. The house was far too large for us of course, but it was a calm and comfortable place to live and the children and I were immediately happy there.

One evening in late August 1924, when we had all been swimming in the river and the twins had gone to bed exhausted by the heat after a day of ceaseless activity, Fizzy and I sat out on the terrace in the evening sunlight and it was there that she dropped her bomb-shell. I had just poured her a glass of wine when out of the blue she asked me whether I loved her. I was not quite sure what she meant so I asked her to explain. To my astonishment tears came to her eyes and she rushed into the house. Alarmed, I followed and found her at the kitchen table with her head on her arms sobbing uncontrollably.

It took me some time to stop her crying and get her to sit up and tell me what the matter was. Through her sobs it all came out. She reminded me that when we were buying my trousseau in London she told me that she did not want to marry anyone other than me 'but that was not allowed'. I felt rather embarrassed. I said something to the effect that I had dismissed what she said because I thought she was just being silly. That provoked more tears but then, when she had regained control of her emotions once more, she explained that she really did love me. She wanted me not just as a friend but as a lover. She knew that I did not feel that way about her and this made her desperately sad.

I felt deeply embarrassed. I did not know what to say. I loved Fizzy as I would have loved a sister, but I most certainly did not want any sort of physical relationship with her. Yet the intensity of her emotions made me sad too and for a while we sat opposite each other at the table in silence neither of us able to speak. Not, mind you, that I could think of anything to say that would not have made matters worse.

It was she who eventually pulled herself together and announced that she would leave the next morning. I tried to protest that it was not necessary for her to go, but she would brook no objections. We passed the rest of the evening in what I suppose you could call an awkward manner, neither of us quite sure what to do or say. I know I felt awful about it all and I imagine that she felt even worse. The next morning when she piled her cases into her car there did not seem to be much to say. All I could manage was to express the hope that she would come back soon. She in turn just said that she was sorry and drove off in a cloud of dust leaving me feeling horribly miserable and confused.

I heard nothing from her for four weeks and then I received a fulsome letter of apology that tried rather unsuccessfully to explain her feelings. Right at the end she said that her father was very ill and this meant that she would not be back in France for some while. I felt rather as if I had been given a brush-off and I felt hurt and confused once more. I wrote back immediately to say how pleased I was to hear from her and how sorry I was about her father. I hoped that what I said would in some way heal the rift that quite clearly had been created by, I have to say, her rather than me.

Four months later, after a total silence during which I had reconciled myself to the possibility that I might not see her again, I received a telegram from my father to tell me that my mother had died and I made frantic plans to return to England. I left the twins with their grandparents and took the earliest possible train to Paris and then London. I had had no time to contact Fizzy before I left home and, indeed, had hesitated to do so because I did not know how she would react. I made up my mind, though, while I was on the Boat Train that I would try to do so, but it was only as I waited at Paddington for my train to Oxford that I plucked up the courage to ring. The butler at Caxton Magna told me that 'Her Ladyship' was in London. I duly tried the house in Belgrave Square, managed to establish that she was indeed staying there but found that she was out. I left a message to say what had happened and where I would be and said I would call again when I reached Oxford. When I next rang her, though, she was still unavailable, so I left another message to say that the funeral was the following afternoon, that I would stay on to be with my father for a few days and hoped she would get in touch. I was disappointed not to have been able to speak to her and found myself wondering whether she was deliberately ignoring my messages. That made me feel sad and a bit guilty. It was the sort of moment when, despite what had happened in the summer, I needed her support and I felt miserable at the thought that she might really no longer wish to be the friend she had been to me.

My father had been in a terrible state when I reached Red Lion

Yard. He was not only desolated by my mother's death but was clearly in poor health himself. It had been more than a year since I had last seen him and I was shocked by the change. He was pathetically pleased to see me and I realised in a flash that without my mother he was a lost man. That made me feel even more guilty. I had chosen to go and live in France and now I could see that I had not been around to care for her in her last days nor for my Father as he grew older. I felt awful as I spent a difficult evening with him while he recounted the saga of mother's last few weeks. He told me that she had insisted that I should not be told and my guilt turned to anger that I was deprived of a last encounter with her.

The funeral was a sombre and upsetting affair. A lot of people turned up and everyone was very nice to me and Father, but nothing anyone said could even remotely penetrate our overwhelming grief. The service passed in a blur and it was only as we filed out to the graveyard that I saw that Fizzy had come. She smiled and gave a discreet wave and, when the coffin had been put in the ground and we turned away from the grave, I found that she was standing close to me. She put an arm around my shoulders, kissed me on the cheek and whispered:

"Oh Dippy darling, I am so, so sorry."

Then she took my arm and together we went out of the churchyard leaving Father to stand alone as the grave-diggers began to replace the soil. As we waited for him to say his solitary farewells, Fizzy plied me with questions about my health and that of the children. Then she asked very quietly whether I had forgiven her for what happened last summer. I told her that of course I had and that I had missed her. That obviously put her at her ease and then Father joined us.

He was clearly flattered that Fizzy should have come to the funeral and was both embarrassed and confused as to how he should play the situation. Fizzy was wonderful, putting him instantly at his ease and then giving him a letter from her father who, she said, had been saddened by the news of Mother's death. By the time we arrived back home where relatives and friends had gathered for the wake, he had regained some of his composure and took obvious pride in introducing her to everyone. Fizzy, for her part, played it absolutely right, avoiding any hint of being grand amongst the hard-working tradespeople who made up my parents' circle of friends.

When the last of them left and Father retired to bed exhausted by the events of recent days, I made Fizzy some supper and we sat at the kitchen table and talked. It was as if nothing had happened between us to upset our friendship. She was her old warm, eccentric self and accepted with alacrity that my affection for her remained as strong as ever, what had happened all those months before notwithstanding. When she left to go back to Caxton Magna, she said that she would come back when I was ready, to take me there too as her father wanted to see me.

The next day I packed Father off to Worcester to stay with his brother for a while, leaving the garage in the hands of his mechanics and then telephoned Fizzy to arrange for her to come to collect me the next afternoon. Then I sat alone in the house and reflected on all that had happened since 1914 when it had been my turn to be packed off to Worcester. As I went to sleep in the darkness in my old bedroom under the eaves that night I could not help smiling to myself as I thought of all that had happened since that strange day.

Waiting for Fizzy I went through my mother's wardrobe and sorted out anything that would quite obviously have no further use. Anything that needed a decision I left for Father to look at first. It was a very moving process because she had obviously hoarded all sorts of objects that were tokens of their love affair and life together. There were also some of my things that she had kept – drawings and childish poems. I felt more grief for her then than I had at the funeral. How strange.

The house looked sad and tawdry. So little had changed from how I remembered it as a child. The horses were gone, of course, and cars and motorcycles had replaced them. The boarding house next door had been closed down when my mother fell ill and I wandered around that wondering what would happen to it. It all depended on what Father wanted, but having seen him so saddened by her death and looking so unwell himself, the thought crossed my mind that it might not be too long before he followed her to the grave. It was a chilling thought and I was so pleased when Fizzy arrived and gave me something else to think about.

When we reached the great house she took me straight away to see her father. He was sitting in a bath-chair in the old library looking old and frail There was a reading stand on one side and a table with medicine bottles on the other. He smiled when he saw me and held out his hand for me to take. He was charm itself.

"Ah Diana, my dear. How good to see. I was so sorry to hear about your mother – a fine woman. My late wife thought the world of her and never really forgave your father for stealing her away."

He paused and looked into the distance and then back at me with a smile.

" Fine groom, George Pink. He was much missed here, I can tell you. I trust he is well."

He stopped and gazed into the distance again.

"I should also say that I was so sorry to hear about your husband. What a terrible accident. I hope you have recovered from the shock and grief."

I told him what I thought necessary about my life since Jean-Paul died and told him, too, that I was worried about Father. I reassured him, I hope, that I was managing well despite the loss of my husband.

"Good, good. Now I wanted to talk to you to say that I have included you in my will. I don't have long for this life my doctor tells me, so I have been busy ensuring that all to whom I feel I owe a debt of gratitude are remembered appropriately."

I went to say something but he waved my protestations away.

"I know I haven't long, my dear. And I can never properly repay you for saving Fiona's life, so you will have to bear with an old man's folly and I hope that my bequest will go some way to expressing my gratitude for all you have done."

He closed his eyes and dozed for a while at this point and I sat there holding his hand until he woke.

"Sorry, my dear. I sleep so much these days. I think it better if you go and find more amusing company. I am so glad to have seen you. May God bless you, Diana, my dear, may God bless you."

It was a dismissal, but the sweetest one he could have given me and as I left the library with tears in my eyes I turned and saw him waving feebly. For all his grandeur and wealth he was a dear man and I felt so sorry to see him eking out his last days alone in that vast house, his wife and his heir dead and aware that in all probability Fizzy would never marry and that therefore the family line would come to an end.

I found Fizzy in one of the loose-boxes and told her what the Duke had said about a bequest. She seemed never to have heard about it but did not seem surprised.

"He's a very generous man, you know, despite living in a world of his own. I am sure he will leave you something nice."

She paused and took my hand, leading me out into the stable-yard.

"I don't think he has long to live, Dippy. I had a word with the doctor the other day after he had paid his weekly visit. I didn't understand the medical jargon but I established that whatever he has is inoperable and will kill him - 'prepare yourself' was what he said as he got into his car."

We walked on out onto the grand terrace at the back of the house.

"The trouble is that when he dies I shall be left with all this."

She waved her arm vaguely in a great sweeping arc.

"And I have no intention of keeping it all. I shall sell it to some rich American with delusions of grandeur and find myself a nice place to live in town. Do you think that would be wrong of me after all these centuries?"

I had no idea what to say and ended up by telling her to do what suited her. There was no line of succession unless she had a son - she snorted derisively at this – and thus no reason why she should feel obliged to shoulder the burden. She kissed me on the cheek and told me that I was so comforting because I was so sensible. That was the end of that.

We drove down to London the next day and I left for France the day after, having telephoned Father in Worcester to see how he was. He sounded very unhappy and begged me to come back to see him as soon as I could. I rang off feeling guilty that I could not stay longer and determined to return in a few weeks.

My intention of returning to England to see Father again was never fulfilled because shortly after I arrived back at La Garenne I received a telegram from my uncle to say that he had died in his sleep within days of arriving to stay with him in Worcester. This coincided almost exactly with another wire from Fizzy informing me that her father had had a massive stroke and was not expected to live long. She asked if I could bear to travel back to England to be with her. She said she was lonely and frightened and needed me.

I wired back to tell her that I was coming anyway and said I would go to Worcester first, then to Oxford for the funeral and finally to Caxton Magna if she could send a car. I then rushed the children back to Monsieur and Madame Dumont and made the arduous journey back to England once again. I spent an uncomfortable night at Uncle William's. My feelings towards him had not changed one jot despite the passage of years and he knew it. I confined myself to talking to the undertakers who would take Father's body back to Oxford for the funeral and to sorting out the personal effects he had brought with him to Worcester. I felt sad and lonely in that hostile house and kept myself to myself. I was hugely relieved when I set off the next morning to accompany the coffin and prepare for the burial.

I was surprised by how many people turned up at the service. They included representatives from the City council, some retired officers from The Oxfordshire Regiment whom he had helped with both horses and vehicles in the War and a number of his customers whose cars he had serviced over the years. I was also amazed to see Fizzy at the back of the church, looking beautiful in black and seemingly moved by the service.

After the burial, a number of people came back to Red Lion Yard to pay their respects to me and it was not until the last of them had gone that I was able to devote any time to Fizzy, who had come too and had helped me with the refreshments provided by a nearby pub. I sank into a chair worn out physically and emotionally. She stood behind me and gently massaged my neck and shoulders. She didn't say anything for a while. Then, sitting down opposite me, she told me how sad she had been at the news of Father's death and how sorry she felt for me. It was a great comfort to have someone to talk to, especially someone who was going through the same experience with her own father. I asked after him and she gave a sad, wry smile and said that it was really only a matter of time. The doctor had now told her that he had an inoperable tumour in his stomach and that the cancer was spreading fast throughout his whole body. He was being very brave but she did not think that he could last more than a few days. We both ended up weeping in the semi-darkness and I do not think I had ever felt closer to her in all the years I had known her. It struck me, when I thought about it later that night, that grief is a great leveller – we had been at that moment just two daughters mourning the loss or the impending loss of a father. I hugged her for a long time as she left to drive back to Caxton Magna.

As I went to close the front door on her I noticed an envelope in the wire cage of the letter box. It had not been there earlier for I recall glancing in that direction for the very purpose of seeing if there had been a postal delivery. Curious, I opened it and found inside a letter from Father's solicitor, who had been amongst the mourners. He must have left it there on his way out of the house. In it he said that he had been approached by a 'certain party' who wished to purchase Father's business and the property. He asked that I call on him the next morning to discuss the terms of the will – of which he said I was the sole beneficiary - and the offer. I went to bed exhausted and as I fell asleep I remember thinking that if I did not sell up I would always have a home in England if I ever wished to return home.

Mr Rutherford, the solicitor, was efficient and businesslike, but not in a way that offended. The will was simple – I inherited everything. There were no debts and a small amount of capital held on deposit at the bank. The offer for the business was a generous one and his advice was that I should accept. If I wished to be an absentee landlord, he said, whilst his firm would be pleased to act for me, he had to warn me that it would be costly to maintain the buildings to an acceptable standard and I might do better to take the money offered and invest it in a more appropriate property or in securities. I told him I would consider the matter and would give him an answer before I left Oxford.

Fizzy sent a car to collect me that evening. By then I had got rid of all Father's clothes and what was left of my Mother's, sorted out his papers, taken the ones that seemed to matter with me and gave the keys of the house to the lady who had been coming in to clean for years. The workshop I left in the safe hands of the head mechanic with instructions that he should defer to Mr Rutherford on anything that required a decision. As I climbed into Lord Dartmoor's Rolls I felt a wave of total sadness wash over me. In a short space of time I had lost both my parents, a devoted couple who had loved me and helped me whenever I needed their support. Now I was leaving the home where I had been born and had grown up, possibly for the last time. I suddenly felt terribly alone and, as I sank back into the rear seats of the great car, I felt sad and lonely. I was still feeling sorry for myself when the car swept through the gates of the great house and deposited me at the front entrance where Dobson, the butler, was waiting to conduct me and my luggage inside.

Fizzy was nowhere to be found so I tracked down the butler again and he told me that she was in the Library with her father. I made to go there and he stopped me.

"His Lordship is in a bad way, Miss Diana. The doctor and a nurse are there too and if I am any judge of the situation I would say that the Duke has not many more hours left on this earth."

He looked genuinely moved as he spoke and I put my hand on his arm. He, in turn, put his hand on mine and smiled tearfully at me.

"I think you are going to hold a lot of hands over the next few hours, Miss. We are all going to need you."

I turned away, moved but also terrified at the weight of responsibility that he seemed to be placing on my shoulders. I was not really in any state myself to help others grieve. I went and sat in the morning room and waited.

Eventually Fizzy came and I could see immediately that something awful had happened. She collapsed into the chair beside mine.

"Oh Dippy darling – you've got to help me. He's dead – he just sighed and that was it. It was so quiet, but also so awful."

She put her head in her hands and wept. I came to sit on the arm of her chair and consoled her as best I could. But I knew from my own experience that no-one can say or do anything at times like this to make things better.

The whole household went to pieces as the news of the Duke's death became known. The outside staff gathered in the stable-yard and waited for someone to go to tell them officially. The indoor contingent gathered in knots to talk in hushed tones. Fizzy was in no state to make any kind of formal statement so, by a sort of process of elimination, it fell to me to do the deed. Mr Dobson summoned everybody to come and stand in the hall below the great staircase and I stood high enough up the stairs so that everyone could see and hear me. He then introduced me as Fizzy's friend and left it to me to say what was needed. I took the view that what everyone wanted were the facts, so that is what I gave them. The death, the cause, the fact that Fizzy was in no state to appear before them and an assurance that as soon as there was any more news to give them I would pass it on. I asked whether there were any questions and one voice from the back demanded to know what would happen to all of them. I am afraid I grew angry at that and snapped back that I did not know any more than I had told them, adding that I thought it a somewhat inappropriate question so soon after their employer had died. This produced a murmur of approval from the assembled group and a lot of glancing back at whoever it was who had asked the question.

When they had dispersed Dobson thanked me and told me that Fizzy had gone up to her room and wanted to see me. I was exhausted by this time and did not relish another emotional session with her, but I went all the same. I found her much calmer. I told what I had done and about the last question I had been asked. She sat up at this and said rather fiercely, I thought, that the future of the house was decided and no-one had anything to worry about. I asked her what she meant and she told me that she had agreed to sell the whole estate and the house in London to an American oil millionaire and as part of the deal he had agreed to take on the staff at both houses.

I must have stared at her in obvious astonishment for she told me, yet again, not to be a silly goose and explained that she had always intended to sell up when her father died. She had been introduced some time ago to the American rejoicing it seemed in the name of Balthazar Caxton Junior, who believed that his family name might imply a historical connection with the house - which, she added, she very much doubted as the place had been in her family long before Columbus discovered America. One thing had led to another and he had ended up offering to buy the place lock stock and barrel for a very large sum of money. She had accepted and, now that her father had died, she intended to go ahead with the deal.

That was it really. The next few days passed in a whirl as I played nurse-maid to Fizzy and then rushed back to Oxford to clear up the legal aspects of my father's death and to sign all the forms to enable Mr Rutherford to sell the property. By the time it came to return to France I was exhausted. Fizzy drove me to London and we stayed the night at Belgrave Square.

There we were visited by the solicitor who was handling the Duke's will. He told me that once probate had been granted and all outstanding matters relating to the estate had been sorted out I, as a beneficiary would be hearing from him again. He told me that Lord Dartmoor had left me something in his will and he handed me a letter from the Duke. I have kept it all these years. This is what it said:

Dear Diana
I am writing this letter in the sure knowledge that before too long I shall have gone to meet my maker. I shall not be sorry – I have had a good life and have been blessed with a happy marriage and two fine children. I am old and ill and want to go to sleep and never awake again. My only regret is that my son is dead and the title dies with me.
You have served me well in your capacity as Fiona's companion. Indeed, you have twice saved her life and that is well beyond the call of duty.
I would like to reward you for this and I am therefore leaving you a small property in Bloomsbury in London, which I bought many years ago and which has been part of my investment portfolio ever since. It produces a reasonable rental income and that will mean that your life, now that you are the sole bread-winner for your family after the tragic loss of your husband, will be more financially secure than it might otherwise have been.
Thank you again, my dear, for all you have done for my daughter.
With every best wish
Dartmoor

The Duke's property turned out to be a small block of flats not far from the British Museum. It consisted of eight flats and these produced an income of over £2000 a year, a fortune by my standards. I was suddenly rich and independent. I could at that moment have done anything I liked, but I chose to go back to France and stay there for the children's sake. Fizzy wrote not long after my return to St Martin to say that the sale of Caxton Magna and all the other properties had gone through for what she called 'a very good price' and she had retained just one cottage on the estate and the mews cottages behind the London house which she intended to turn into a house.

She said something in that letter that intrigued me. Apparently someone had told her that he was worried about the the economic situation in both America and England and had suggested that she sell all her father's investments and put all her money into gold. She admitted that she did not understand what it was all about but trusted the man concerned and had indeed sold everything, bought some property in Westminster and put the rest into bullion.

On my side, the sale of my father's property in Oxford went through and I found that I had over £2000 pounds to invest. On Fizzy's advice I bought two small houses in north London to let. With the rent from them and the income from Lord Dartmoor's flats I was rich. I had no idea what I would do with my new-found wealth, but I enjoyed the thought of it.

So life went on. The business did well, the twins grew into healthy, intelligent children and my existence was bearable despite the continuing sense of loss I had felt since Jean-Paul died. I was not exactly unhappy. It was more that I was unfulfilled despite living in a beautiful house and having no money worries. Even though nearly ten years had passed since the end of the War, I still felt that, despite the danger and the appalling amount of death and destruction I had witnessed, life then had been exhilaratingly exciting. The children were a compensation of course and I watched them grow with delight. Marie was the quicker and smarter of the two. Poor Charles always seemed to be one step behind her and, whilst he did not seem to care, it worried me that this might prove to be a disadvantage in adult life.

Fizzy was a great support. As well as writing to me regularly she would appear at La Garenne from time to time unannounced and invariably in yet another exotic car. I did not mind. It was clear that she needed to see me and for my part I was always grateful for the companionship she brought, for she was, in truth, my only real friend. Jean-Paul's family, though I saw a lot of them, were never people in whom I could confide.

Down in our part of France we were not much affected by the Great Crash when it came. Fizzy's rich American, though, lost all his money and abandoned Caxton Magna. She wrote about it with what I felt was unseemly glee. Poor man: whatever his vain delusions about his family origins, I could not join her in celebrating his fall from grace.

During the 1930s, with the children attending the Lycée in Périgueux, I devoted myself to running the company and to my horses. The sense of a lack of fulfilment remained and it took Fizzy and my son Charles between them to provide the solution. Fizzy, for her part had started to write rather alarmingly about concerns in London over what was happening in Germany. She was well-connected to the circle of people around Winston Churchill, who, she said, was convinced that Hitler's rise to power meant that Britain could find itself at war with her old enemy again, possibly within the next two or three years. I wrote back saying that I was shocked to hear this, especially after the horrors we had seen for ourselves, but I knew that if there was to be another war then I would prefer to be in England not France.

My mind was made up not by Fizzy though, but by Charles, who by chance came home from school one weekend and said that he wanted to know more about England. I had always brought him up to feel that he was half French and half British and he said that he had been talking to his teacher who had said disparaging things about 'Les Anglais' and he wanted to see for himself. Marie was less interested – she had her horse and friends in the village and was more content with her lot. In the end I persuaded her that it would be a good thing to go to see what it was like and in the end we agreed that we would go there during the long summer holiday.

Fizzy was delighted to hear this and said she would drive down to collect us. Thus it was that in mid-July 1937 I found myself sitting beside her in yet another amazing car, this time a rather beautiful blue Lagonda. The children sat in the back and I think they were completely flabbergasted by the experience. We roared through France at great speed and in two days, with an overnight stop near Paris, we were in London. We stayed with Fizzy at the house in Belgrave Mews and we spent the first two days showing them the sights. Then we drove down to Oxford to show them where I was born. The old garage, which of course was nothing much more than a converted stables, had gone and in its place there was a modern workshop. Bert Foster, the mechanic who used to work for Father was now in charge and the whole place looked prosperous and flourishing. I was glad, though I could not help feeling a little sad to see that what had been my childhood home had effectively disappeared. We went finally to Caxton Magna, which had now stood empty for some years after Mr. Caxton's bankruptcy. It looked very sad and I felt a real pang of regret, not least for all the staff there who had presumably lost their jobs. Fizzy told me that she had done what she could for them and continued to help anyone in real difficulty. She looked sad though and, I think, a bit guilty.

I was taken to meet the current command at the FANY headquarters in Grosvenor Crescent who welcomed me warmly. They all seemed to know about Fizzy's and my exploits in France during the war and they treated us as special people, which was flattering and nice. I was also taken to meet a man who had been tasked by Mr Churchill to put in place lines of communications to all sorts of people so that, if war did break out with Hitler's Germany, at least he, if no-one else, would be able to move quickly and activate cells whose sole objective would be to frustrate anything the Germans might have put in place themselves to penetrate the British government. Nothing was said to me specifically, but I assumed that when the time came I could be called upon to act in some role or other.

The children loved London, far more than I thought they would. The largest town they knew was Périgueux and they were clearly amazed at the scale of such a city. It was a voyage of discovery for me, too, because my knowledge of the place was limited to what I had seen and done in the wake of Fizzy's various progresses around town years before. I found it fascinating, but I confess I soon started to miss La Garenne, my horses and the slower pace of country life.

On our return to France the children continually pestered me to take them to London again. Marie, in particular, wanted to live there. Charles was less sure, but he agreed with his sister that he now wanted more out of life than what the Dordogne could offer them. I argued that they would find it a strange environment in which to live and that they would miss the countryside and the climate, but to no avail. I did nothing, thinking they would soon find something else to distract them.

Then out of the blue in 1938 I received an offer from one of the large transport outfits with a head office in Paris to buy my company. My immediate reaction was to say no. I had enjoyed building up the firm and it was now a success and gave me great satisfaction. Then the thought occurred to me that as the twins were approaching the age of eighteen and would leave home soon, perhaps there was something to be said for selling up and doing something else with my life. The upshot was that I agreed to meet and discuss the possibility of selling Transports Dumont after all. Negotiations proved to be easy and I got my way on everything I demanded. They even agreed to pay my price which was a good deal higher than their opening bid and they promised me that they would keep my staff and honour my commitments to what had been a loyal and effective workforce.

Thus in the middle of the year I found myself a rich woman with nothing much to occupy my time. I decided that perhaps after all we might go and live in England for a while. My parents-in-law had both died the year before and the Dumont properties had already been divided according to the Code Napoleon between me as Jean-Paul's widow, his children and his siblings. The house in the village was now occupied by his older brother, Henri, who farmed the family land. Our portion was a house in the village which was let and some land that abutted La Garenne which I allowed Henri to use. His sister and brother-in-law, who lived in Poitiers, had chosen to take the house in Nontron that old Monsieur Dumont had inherited from his parents and they let it to the manager of the local bank.

As for the horses, over the years I had focused more and more on the 'talking' side of things and had gradually given up breeding them. That meant that I could simply stop what I was doing and, as it were, shut up shop. Apart from the house at La Garenne there was little for me to worry about and I therefore decided that I would store anything of value that we were not taking with us and brick up good old Boanerges so that he was hidden from any prying eyes that might invade the privacy of our barns while we were away. Towards the end of September 1938 we packed our boxes and trunks into a lorry that would carry them to England, I locked up the house and we left, confident that when we returned it would still be in good order.

We reached London on 30 September after a night in Paris. I confess I was as excited as the twins by the time we arrived in England, especially as Fizzy had insisted that we live in one of her flats in Ashley Gardens that had unexpectedly fallen vacant. She met the Boat Train at Victoria, transported us back to her house for the first night and our adventure began. It was there that I listened to Neville Chamberlain on the radio declaring that he had returned from his talks with Hitler and that there would be 'peace in our time'. I can still remember Fizzy's snort of derision when she heard these words.

"Stupid old fool! There'll be war, Dippy. You mark my words."

I little knew then how right she was.

For the first week we did nothing but look at the sights. Fizzy took us everywhere and entertained us as if we were visiting royalty. It really was, as I have said, an adventure: we went to the theatre, something neither I nor the children had ever done before. We went to a cinema – again something we had never done, and to museums and art galleries. It was seven days of one wonderful experience after another.

At first I thought no-one else but Fizzy was worried about the chances of war breaking out again, but then, after we had been in London for a while she started to introduce me to her friends almost all of whom were convinced that it was only a matter of time before something would have to be done about the Nazis. From what they said I began to see that it was not just a question of righting what Germans perceived to be the unfairness of their treatment after the 1914-18 War, but of Hitler wishing to impose a new order on Europe, which was unacceptable. At the same time I began to hear about his treatment of Jews, their persecution and the rounding up and dispatch to camps of those accused of being opponents of Germany. At the time no-one was really aware of the horrors that hid behind the gates of those camps, but the mere thought of a system that threatened to spread its police state rule over other parts of Europe horrified many people.

Fizzy took me to meet the FANY commanders and I volunteered my services should they ever be needed. They were mainly involved in transport matters it seemed. The old Nursing Yeomanry mantle had gone, largely as a result, I was told, of the integration of the Corps into the Auxiliary Transport Service, which is what the female branch of the Army was called. I got the distinct feeling that the FANYs were unhappy with this, but no-one told me as much. It was Fizzy who let the cat out of the bag, of course. She told me that many of her fellow FANYs were determined that they would not be treated as fit for nothing better than being drivers or mechanics.

Marie had been found a place at what Fizzy called a 'finishing school' where, in addition to attending classes, she was to be taught what I suppose you would call the social graces, something I was the first to admit was not part of the school curriculum in rural France nor something that I had ever been taught. Charles had found himself a place at a college in Holborn that promised to help him pass his accountancy exams if he was prepared to work hard. So, with Marie suddenly in what turned out to be a madly social milieu, which gave her a collection of new friends, and with my son seemingly dedicated to the task of getting a qualification, I was free to see what London had to offer me.

Fizzy gave a cocktail party to launch me, as she put it, and there I met a pilot whom I liked very much even though at the age of forty-one and a widow with two children I think I had written off the idea of having a love life again. Archie Hobbs was a year younger than me and a veteran of the Royal Flying Corps which he had joined in 1917. A handsome, tall, sandy haired man with very blue eyes, he had transferred to the RAF when it was formed in 1918 in the last months of the war and after the armistice he had opted to stay on as a regular officer. He had become a Hurricane pilot when they came into service and was based down at Tangmere in Sussex where he was responsible for training new pilots to fly the plane. He was very amusing and, as I discovered later that evening when he bore me away to a nightclub, a wonderful dancer. After years of dedicated widowhood I found that I was falling in love again.

Archie was amazing. When he was not flying he would come up to London to take me dancing and out to dinner. My head began to spin with the romance of it all. He even took me up in a little plane, which I found terrifying but amazingly exhilarating. I could not get out of my mind the sight of the aircraft in which Jean Paul crashed. But at the same time I loved speeding over the English countryside with the wind roaring in my ears. By the end of three weeks I was hopelessly infatuated. Fizzy was disapproving, but I suspect this was because she was jealous of Archie and, perhaps, of me. But to her credit she did not let that show and always greeted him warmly whenever she met him with me.

Archie was one of those who was convinced that there would be a war. "It's only a matter of time" was what he always said whenever he was asked. He had been fully behind Churchill in his campaign to persuade the government to re-arm as quickly as possible and he was concerned that foot-dragging in Whitehall would put Britain at a disadvantage as and when the moment came.

Our romance blossomed quickly and soon became physical. I confess that I had never really thought of myself as desirable in sexual terms, even though Jean Paul had always told me that I was beautiful, but Archie made me feel like a goddess. Over the weeks that followed the first time we went to bed together both he and I were insatiable lovers. So much so that not only Fizzy noticed it but the children too. Fizzy was jealous and sulked for a while. Marie was intensely curious about what was going on. Charles was unsettled to find that his mother had eyes for someone other than him and his sister.

My love for Archie grew as I got to know him better. He was not a man of many words but he was clearly inspired by flying. He once said to me that flight was a very spiritual thing . "When you're up there you feel close to God or eternity or whatever you like to call it." I can still remember him saying that to me and when he took me up again for what he called a 'spin' in a little Gypsy Moth biplane I knew instantly what he meant. It was so unreal to be floating high up above the green fields with the man I loved. I can still remember the feeling all these years afterwards. It was so completely overwhelming it was almost sexy. I know that later that day we made love more passionately than ever before.

By the middle of 1939 we seemed to have settled down into a pattern of life that everyone found agreeable. Marie had an active social life, having been swept up by the other girls at the school and introduced to their friends. Charles worked hard at his studies and had found a good friend at the college called Danny Parsons. They were rather similar young men – both shy and awkward with girls. They both loved football and cricket and in the winter of 1938 Danny took Charles to watch some of the London teams. The next summer Fizzy had arranged with a friend in the MCC for the boys to have special passes for Lords so that they could go and watch whenever they wanted. Fizzy got me more involved with the FANYs and we were both assigned to drive senior members of the the armed forces. I really enjoyed this and I met all sorts of interesting people that way.

As the summer came to an end the mood in London grew much more sombre. Germany's intentions towards Poland were clearly hostile and although there was a lot of speechifying about it, I could tell from the way the people I drove were talking that no-one really thought that Hitler would modify his plans just because the British and the French were thumping the table. On the fateful morning of September the 3rd I was one of a crowd of drivers huddled round a radio at the War Office to hear the Prime Minister announce that Britain had declared war on Germany. I can still hear the absolute silence that greeted his words and then the noise as everyone spoke at once. It was one of the most chilling moments in my life: I had lived through the horrors of the last war and now we were going to do it again.

I did not see Archie again for some days. All leave had been cancelled for his Squadron and, while he assured me that it was very unlikely that he would have to fly any missions for the time being, everyone had been put on full war footing. I noticed the change in Whitehall too. Sandbags appeared everywhere and we were all issued with gas-masks. The tension was horrible. It was made worse for me by the fact that Charles came home a few days later and informed me that he and Danny had joined up and that he had been immediately given a commission and posted to a unit created to liaise with the French. I was frightened by the sudden turn of events and I now had to fear not only for Archie's safety but for my son's too.

Charles was assigned very soon after that to the British Expeditionary Force and sent to France to act as an interpreter at headquarters. Marie talked of joining up but did nothing about it. Fizzy was put in charge of one of the ATS transport units. I carried on driving people around but I registered with the FANYs the fact that I could speak fluent French thinking that there might be a role for me somewhere that needed the language. Archie flew patrols over the Channel but reported that nothing was happening. What we started to call the 'phoney war' had begun. It was a very strange time to be in London. Things went on much as before, but hanging over everyone was a feeling of genuine fear.

I saw as much of Archie as I could because I knew that he could be killed at any time. I loved having him with me and hated it when he had to fly. I knew that he would seek out danger – that is what made him so good at his job. But I also knew that in courting death he was tempting fate and that one day he would run out of luck. That was something I dreaded. We used to drive down to Fizzy's cottage at Caxton Magna whenever he had enough time to spare and we took to walking in the grounds of the neglected house. It made me sad to see so much grandeur gone to ruins. I used to tell him about my adventures with her in the last war. I think he thought I was mad, but I think he also rather enjoyed hearing what I had done with my life. They were happy times, not least because the threat that hung over our heads all the time made it all the more important that we should have fun together. I used to love racing around the country lanes in his little Hillman convertible – which he called 'The Bus' - with the hood down and the wind in my hair. It sounds awful to say it but it was very much a case of 'eat, drink and be merry for tomorrow we may die'.

In early June 1940 Archie drove up to town from Tangmere to tell me that all the signs were, as he put it, that the balloon was about to go up. We spent the evening together dancing at the Cafe de Paris and then he came back to flat and stayed until dawn. I hated saying goodbye to him because I was aware every time I did so that it could be for the last time. In fact the Germans held off their attack until the middle of the month and, while the British had eventually to withdraw towards Calais, the German guns were directed at the poor Dutch and Belgians. Archie continued to fly patrols and told me that German ships seemed to be more numerous in the Channel but he had few encounters with enemy fighter planes.

Then at the end of the month everything fell apart. The Germans literally pushed us into the sea and those who could not be evacuated by the huge flotilla of little boats that came to their rescue were captured. Charles was among those seized by the Germans, having been part of the liaison group that stayed behind with the French forces. At the time I feared he could be dead, but was soon re-assured that he was not and, after a very long time, I received a letter about him sent by the Red Cross which told me that he was safe, well and in a German prisoner of war camp.

Amazingly Archie seemed able to lead a charmed life. Despite almost endless sorties as bombers poured across The Channel he escaped serious harm, though he told me once that he had had several planes badly shot up. I began to relax about him believing that he would in fact survive the terrible battle that I could see being fought in the skies above me. But then on the fifteenth of September the Luftwaffe launched a huge raid on London. It was the most terrifying day of my life. Bombers darkened the sky as they dropped their dreadful cargo of explosives on the city. There were fires everywhere and the smell of smoke and the sound of sirens and of people shouting blotted out any sensible thought. It seemed that at any moment any one could die. Everyone was nervous and there was a good deal of anxious telephoning. I managed to get through to Marie and made sure that she was all right and she reassured me that she would be home as soon as she could get away. She sounded as frightened as the rest of us.

I did not know then of the efforts the RAF were making to defeat this massive attack. Only when the bombers turned tail and flew back to Europe did the news emerge that our pilots had out-flown and out-fought the Luftwaffe and had repulsed them. Like most of the other drivers at The War Office, I was euphoric until I thought about Archie. Then an awful sense of foreboding came over me and when, late that afternoon the phone rang in the flat, I knew in my bones before I answered it that it was the call I had been dreading for months.

Archie's friend Mike tried so hard to soften the blow but in the end the news he had rung to give me was as bad as it could be however it was voiced. My darling Archie was dead. His had been a hero's death, Mike said. He had shot down five enemy planes and then, when his own had been hit and was on fire, he had deliberately crashed it into another German bomber killing himself in the process but downing over the Channel a full load of bombs destined for London.

I could not say anything other than to thank him before I had to put the phone down. I then sat down and cried and cried. It seemed that fate was destined to take from me any man I loved. My mind kept going over all the wonderful moments we had had together, the fun, the thrills and, it has to be said, the love-making. I lost track of time as I wept while I recalled everything. It was only the persistent ringing of the telephone that eventually brought me out of my reverie. It was Marie, who had been unable to travel home because of the disruption the bombing had caused and was concerned to know whether I was all right. I gave her the news about Archie. There was a long pause before she said anything and when she did speak I could tell that she, too, was crying. Through her sobs she tried to commiserate with me.

"Oh Maman – I am so, so sorry. I shall be home as soon as I can."

I sat by the phone thanking God that I had a daughter who cared for her mother.

Then the phone rang again and woke me once more from my reverie. This time it was Fizzy. Marie had rung her as soon as she had spoken to me and told her the news and to ask Fizzy to go to me immediately in case she had difficulty getting home as quickly as she would like. She told me she was on her way to me and before I could protest that I wanted to be alone, she had rung off. By then the full impact of Archie's death hit me and I must have collapsed onto my bed and slept, because I woke up to find Marie standing beside me looking concerned with Fizzy, whose arrival had coincided with hers, hovering in the background. As I woke they plied me with advice and questions in equal measure.

I know they meant well, but I did not want their ministrations. I just wanted to be by myself to mourn, just as I had done when Jean-Paul died. The death of someone you love is such a personal thing: no-one else can minimise the grief nor can anyone point you to a way out of the painful process of coming to terms with the situation. Fizzy suggested that a strong drink would help, Marie proposed that we just talk about it. Neither idea appealed one jot, but it took me some while to persuade them that all I wanted was to be alone. When they eventually left me in my room in the dark, I cried again and tried to relive the happiness I had known with Archie.

I spent a disturbed night slipping in and out of nightmares that were interspersed with periods during which I was entirely calm and slept deeply. By morning my anger had abated and the sadness that I had felt with it had also gone. In their place was a determination to do something to hit back. So far my war had been a passive thing. I had reacted to circumstances and to that extent I had done my bit, but now, having lost so much of what mattered to me, I felt able to consider putting my own life at risk to avenge the harm that had been done to me and my family.

I forced myself to go back to work the next day, thinking it would be better to keep busy than to have time to dwell on things. I was surprised to find myself assigned a week later to a new department called The Inter-Services Research Bureau with an office in Baker Street. When I arrived there I was signed in with a great deal of fuss as my credentials were checked and then I was conducted upstairs to a waiting room and told that someone called Miss Atkins would see me shortly. I little knew, then, that this would be the beginning of an extraordinary departure for me. Vera Atkins turned out to be a formidable lady with an aquiline nose and a forbidding, rather haughty manner who wore the uniform of a WAAF officer. As soon as I was shown into her room she spoke to me in fluent if slightly accented French and we used that language for the best part of ten minutes. Then, out of the blue she switched to English, which she spoke with the same slight accent.

"Very good, Madame Dumont - excellent. I think you will do very well."

I confess I stood there looking at her in amazement. No-one in London had called me 'Madame' since my return. I could not think what was going on. Eventually I stammered something like "do for what?" and waited for her to enlighten me. I could feel myself blushing.

She sat back in her chair and motioned me to sit down.

"I am sorry. I thought you knew who and what we are here. Clearly you do not. That is regrettable."

She then sat back put her fingers together, rested her chin on them and looked at me again for some while.

"You are at the headquarters of the Special Operations Executive. My superior, Colonel Buckmaster, and I run F Section which is responsible for operations in France. Your name was passed to us by a member of the FANY as someone who knew France well, who had proved herself in dangerous circumstances and who could be trusted to keep secrets."

She then explained in some detail the origins of SOE, its

objectives and its requirements. She laid huge stress on the secrecy of the operation, saying that any breach of security could endanger many lives. She then asked me whether I would be prepared to come and work for her and to help train agents who were to be sent to France to support The Resistance there.

I needed no time to consider how I should respond and accepted there and then. This was the answer to my prayers. I needed something that would blot out my sadness at the loss of Archie, something more demanding than driving people around London, something to help me forget poor Charles languishing in a POW camp and, above all, something to give a meaning to the senselessness of the ghastly war I was living through. I asked Miss Atkins to tell me who had told her about me. She smiled.

"There's nothing mysterious about that. You were recommended by a good friend of yours whom I have met from time to time – Lady Moretonhampstead. I was saying at dinner one evening a few weeks ago that I needed to find people who really knew France to help me with training and she immediately suggested you. She told me some impressive things about your experiences in the last war. I made some checks and here we are!"

I think I knew it had to be Fizzy!

I was posted to work at the training school at Wanborough Manor near Guildford to gain experience of the organisation. It was exciting, even though it was also extremely demanding. The mood there was exhilarating – it was not just the courage of the 'students' who came through there, but the genuine belief that they, with our help, could really do something to help win the war. After a while, after I had then been sent on a basic training course which included a parachute drop, unarmed combat and weapons training, I was moved down to Beaulieu in the New Forest where I became intimately involved with the final briefings for agents to be sent to France. It was so important that they did nothing to betray themselves when near Germans - especially the Gestapo who were, we were told, constantly on the look out for agents who had been infiltrated into France from 'enemy' territory. We pushed them hard and from time to time someone would fail and be told that they did not have the right qualities for operational work. By the end of April 1941 some of the agents we had trained were deemed ready to be sent behind the lines and the first of them was dispatched in May. We were not told any details for security reasons – security was always paramount as you can imagine – but there was a buzz of excitement as the news inevitably filtered through. I felt proud to be associated, even though in a very humble way with such a courageous enterprise. My only sadness was that many of the agents were flown on what were called the 'Black' flights to France in Lysanders which took off from Tangmere airfield, a constant reminder of my lost lover.

There was not much to do in my spare time apart from enjoy the beauty of the house and parkland at Beaulieu. Occasionally there was a chance of a lift up to London and when that happened I used to go to see Marie and then spend some time with Fizzy. London was such a strange place after the peace and quiet of Hampshire and while I enjoyed the change of environment it inevitably brought back memories of the good times I had spent with Archie and that made me sad. Marie was still very busy doing her liaison work but told me very little about what she actually did. I had become used to the fact that in war-time people did not talk about their work, but I would have loved to have known more. In fairness, I told her nothing about what I did so perhaps it was only reasonable of her to withhold the information from me. With Fizzy I was no more forthcoming even though, as a FANY, she was herself part of an organisation from whose ranks a number of the people we trained came and she knew Vera Atkins and many of the people associated with her. This became a bone of contention between us for a while until I managed to persuade her that I really could not tell her anything about what I as doing because I had sworn a solemn oath not to do so. She very reluctantly accepted this but remained sulky for some time afterwards. Sometimes she could be exasperatingly petulant, I suppose because she was a still at heart a spoiled rich girl.

As for Archie, there seemed to be reminders of him wherever I went and whoever I met and my broken heart refused to mend. The worst moment I think was when his old Commanding Officer contacted me to tell me that his bravery on the day he died was to be marked by the award of a posthumous DFC and he asked whether I would like be the person who received it from the King. I said that there must surely be a relative who could do that and he told me that there was no-one they could find despite a great deal of effort. They had concluded that he did not have any living relatives. I realised then that he had never talked about his family. I accepted that they must all be dead and agreed to go to the Palace on his behalf. I did so with a heavy heart though. I had tried so hard to put his death into some sort of backwater of my mind and to have to be reminded of it in such a highly charged environment would, I knew, re-awaken many painful memories. I asked if I might bring Marie with me. The CO said he was sure that would be possible and he would see what he could do. A week later a crested white envelope arrived from something called rather grandly The Central Chancery of the Order of the Knighthood. It contained two rather dull-looking beige tickets inviting Marie and me to attend an investiture at Buckingham Palace at the end of October 1941.

The same day to my delight and enormous relief I received a letter via the Red Cross from Charles. I knew that after he had been captured at Dunkirk he had been taken to Germany, but I had no idea where he was being held or how he was. His letter which was obviously written under extreme constraint simply told me that he was well, that he had access to some books provided by the Red Cross and was studying accountancy with the help of a fellow prisoner. He sent his love to me and Marie. That is all. I can remember so clearly even now how, though I felt a wave of total relief, I felt close to tears for what seemed like hours. I telephoned Marie to give her the news and to say that I would be coming up to Town at the weekend. She promised to come to see me. Then I phoned Fizzy who insisted that I come to stay with her so that she could celebrate the news with some champagne she had hidden away for a special occasion.

In the end neither of these things happened. I was suddenly very busy at Beaulieu and had to put Marie off and it was Fizzy who cancelled our date saying mysteriously that she had to go away for a while. She would not be drawn on where she was going nor why saying only that she would tell me when we next met.

When I next went up to London I learned that Fizzy had been to America and back, which was why she had cancelled our date. She told me that she had been asked to act as a courier delivering some papers to the The British Joint Staff Mission in Washington. I expressed my surprise that she should have been chosen for such a job. She laughed and said something about knowing people in high places and I was reminded of our encounter with the man she called Uncle Bun, the General we had met in London in 1914. She then completely astounded me by saying that she was going to be sent back to Washington very shortly to join the Mission on a permanent basis. When I asked why, she laughed again and said that it was because the Americans loved people with titles and Churchill liked to exploit that whenever he could. I did not understand and, to be honest, I still don't – but yet again it demonstrated that, much as I loved her as a friend, her world and mine were still sometimes miles apart.

I did not see Marie. I had no idea where she was and my enquiries proved useless. I was puzzled and I confess that having returned to Beaulieu without having seen her I wrote a rather curt letter saying that I was disappointed that she could not spare her mother time and hoped very much that she would not forget to come to Buckingham Palace with me. I had an immediate response: she telephoned the next evening to say how sorry she was but she had been deeply involved with something else and was unable to let me know. She promised to be at the investiture. I asked what it was that prevented her from meeting me, but all she would say was that she had been on an assignment which she couldn't talk about. I was used to that sort of thing, so did not press her.

I did not see her again until we went together to the Palace. She seemed different, more mature and more pensive. I did not give it much thought at the time: the war had changed all of us in so many ways. I presented the tickets to the policeman on duty at the gates and he waved us through into the great courtyard. We followed the line of people making their way into the building and along carpeted corridors lined with grand portraits until we found ourselves being shown to our seats in what the young serviceman who found us our places said was the Ballroom. It was a very grand place, crowded with men and women, mostly in uniform, who were presumably there to receive decorations, accompanied by their families. At the far end of the room was a raised dais and eventually the King and Queen emerged from one side and took their places there.

Names were called and the recipients of honours went one by one to meet His Majesty as their citations were read out. When Archie's turn came a young soldier came to conduct me to the dais where the King handed me the leather box containing his medal. I was overcome by the splendour of the occasion and also the incredible sadness of the moment and I could not stop a tear running down my face. As I shook the King's hand and turned to go back to my seat the Queen smiled sympathetically at me and I heard her say quietly "I am so sorry my dear."

That was it: we sat there and watched the procession of brave men and women plus a few sorrowing bereaved like me until all the medals had been handed out. Then we made our way into an ante-room before being shown the way back to the great gates and out into The Mall in the autumn sunshine. I felt completely drained by the whole thing and was at a loss to know what to do next. To my surprise Marie took charge and marched me up Constitution Hill to Hyde Park Corner. From there we turned into Halkin Street and walked towards Belgrave Square. I suddenly realised that we were close to Fizzy's house and to my astonishment that is exactly where my daughter was taking me. Fizzy was waiting with the champagne she had promised me before to celebrate the life of my darling Archie and I have to say that after a couple of glasses of the wine my sorrow seemed to vanish and we spent the afternoon happily remembering him. I felt almost ashamed to leave the house at dusk in such high spirits.

That did not last long though, because as Marie and I walked back to Ashley Gardens she said that there was something that she wanted to tell me, adding that she should not do so but wanted me to know. Puzzled I told her to go ahead and she duly dropped her bombshell.

" Maman – I am going back to France."

I remember stopping dead in my tracks and just staring at her. I told her I did not understand to which she retorted that I should because I was involved in sending people back to France. My first reaction was to wonder how on earth she knew that, but then the penny dropped – she must have been recruited by SOE. I was so shocked that I did not know what to say and it was not until I had physically marched her back to the flat and sat her down in front of me that I was able to come to my senses and ask her calmly and, I hoped, affectionately what exactly she was trying to tell me.

She told me that someone had apparently recommended her to F Section and she had been called in to talk to Vera Atkins. Vera had quickly worked out that she was my daughter and had told her what I was doing. She was instructed that if that complicated things then she was free to decline the offer of a chance to return to the country of her birth and do what she could to help the resistance movement. Marie, being a fiercely independent sort of girl had said that my work with SOE did not in her view complicate matters. She would be delighted to do what she could and all she asked was that she be allowed to tell me about it. Vera had told her that as it was likely that she would come across me anyway there was no objection, but she had stressed the need otherwise to keep the whole thing to herself. This she had promised to do.

I did not know what to say. The thought of her being parachuted into enemy territory filled me with dread, but I knew that if I had been her I would not have given the matter a second thought. I would have accepted on the spot. That, of course, is what she in fact had done. She told me that she would go even if I objected. In the face of that determination I could but give my blessing, even though I did so with a heavy heart. I knew so well the dangers our people ran and I was aware that the Germans were cunning and successful in identifying and eliminating the resistance and, in particular, foreign agents.

When I left her at the flat to catch my train back to Beaulieu, I did so feeling sad. With my son a POW, my lover dead and now my daughter about to depart on what was probably a suicidal mission, I needed desperately to talk to someone and on the spur of the moment instead of heading to the station I retraced my steps back to Fizzy's house praying that she would be there.

I rang the doorbell long and hard but no-one came. I tried knocking and still no response. I was just about to leave and make my way to the station when an army staff car pulled into the mews and stopped beside me. I heard Fizzy's voice wishing the driver good night and she emerged from the back in uniform and carrying a large briefcase.

When she saw me she put down the case and threw her arms around me.

"Oh Dippy darling – what on earth has happened. I thought you had to be back in the country tonight ."

She gave me no chance to explain. Instead she ushered me in and sat me down in the kitchen. Standing in front of me she then demanded to know what the matter was and why I looked so pale and shocked. Throwing caution to the winds, knowing that I really should protect Marie's mission rather than spread the word, I told her everything. When I had finished she said nothing for a while. Then, sitting down at the table opposite me, she reached over and took my hand and looked me in the eye.

"Do you realise, my darling Dippy, that what Marie is doing is no more than what you did when you got off that train in 1914. You can't stop her and if you tried she would find a way a of going. She is brave girl, just like her mother and, though it's horribly dangerous, she must be allowed to go."

She insisted that I stay the night. I telephoned to tell the people down in Hampshire that I had been detained in London and would be back the next morning. We then spent the evening talking, drinking a bit too much than was good for us and feasting on a tin of ham that she had somehow obtained from some Canadian officers she was friendly with. Looking back I have no doubt that that was the best thing for me. Had I returned to Beaulieu immediately after Marie told me her news I would have been in such a turmoil. As it was, though I was still desperately frightened for her, I knew that Fizzy was right and that I had to let her accept the assignment.

Fizzy left for America soon after that and I did not see her again until late in 1942. By then of course America had entered the war after Pearl Harbour and Marie had been sent to France. Mercifully I was not involved with her training and final briefings. It would have been too much for me and I imagine that F Section realised that. I did see her before she went though. We met in London and had a very tense and emotional parting. I dreaded the thought that it could be the last time I would ever see her. I think she felt the same and by the time we each went our different ways all we could do was cling to each other wordlessly and then walk away without looking back.

For the next year I worked as hard as I could to try to keep myself from worrying about Marie and, of course, Charles – though I was reassured that as a prisoner he was at least likely to be safe even if he was suffering. Fizzy I only saw once in all that time. She had to fly back to London as a courier with some important papers and she telephoned me and we met hurriedly. She was her usual self, having a wonderful time in Washington it seemed. It was a real tonic to see her and I felt so much better to have a real friend to talk to just for once. Not that my colleagues at Beaulieu were in any way unfriendly: it was just that we had become so used to not talking about things that we even managed not to talk about ourselves. Fizzy's message to me about Marie was that no news had to be good news and I had but to agree.

The bad news did come in the end though, as I had always known it would. One day in March 1944 Vera Atkins paid a visit to our training centre and towards the end of her inspection she asked to see me. I think I knew even before she spoke that she was going to tell me what I had dreaded hearing for so long. Indeed, I pre-empted her. When I came into the room I simply said "She's dead, isn't she?"

She did not answer me immediately, but waited for me to take the seat to which she had waved me. Then she looked me in the eye and simply said "Yes."

She waited a while and then she took my hand and said very gently.

"I'm so sorry Diana, so very, very sorry."

Then she gave me a while to come to terms with the reality and to compose myself. It was me who finally broke the silence.

"How did it happen and when and where?"

"I do not have the full story yet, I'm afraid, but I shall tell you all that I do know. You will not be aware that she was assigned to one of our circuits in central France. She performed magnificently well, as a wireless operator and, when required, acting as a courier to take messages to outlying cells and to other circuits. It was on one of the latter missions that she was caught. She had gone down to Angoulême on the train with a message for the leader of a small group we have at Champniers. It seems that she was recognised getting off the train by someone from your old village who had become a member of the Milice. He told a Gestapo officer at the station and she was arrested by the Germans. She was taken back to a village called St Martin-sur-Force, which is I think where she grew up, and the identification was confirmed. After interrogation, under which I am told she was amazingly brave and gave nothing away, I am afraid that she was then sentenced to death and executed in public as an example to any one else in the community who might, as they put it 'be collaborating with the enemy'. I am afraid that I know no more than that."

Even though I had always known that this could happen, when the moment came it was too much to bear. Miss Atkins waited patiently while my grief overwhelmed me and it was some time before I could ask her whether there was any clue as to the identity of the man who recognised her. All she could tell me was that he had lived in the village and had been to school with her.

When she had gone I was told that she had ordered that I be given compassionate leave. Instead of staying in London where there was no-one now to whom I could turn, I went back to Beaulieu and contented myself by riding my bicycle in the New Forest each day until I was so tired I was able to fall asleep immediately rather than lie awake imagining what had happened to my darling daughter.

I returned to work after ten days a changed woman. My objective now was to somehow get myself to France so that I could work out how I might avenge Marie's death by finding the man who betrayed her and killing him, but that proved easier said than done. While we did not know about the coming invasion of France, it was clear to all of us that something was going to happen and though I tried my hardest to be sent as a courier to one of the resistance groups who would act in support of the invasion by disrupting Nazi movements, I failed utterly.

In the end I had to wait until after the Germans surrendered in May 1945 before I was able to get myself to somewhere near home and thus capable of taking my revenge if I could. I heard that they were looking for interpreters to work with a bomb disposal team being sent to destroy caches of explosives and weapons that had not been used by the resistance groups to which they had been sent. I volunteered and no objection was made back at Baker Street. We flew to Bordeaux and travelled to near Royan where the Germans had held out grimly against the Allies after D-Day. We then moved eastwards from cache to cache neutralising those that we could find and recording those that had somehow disappeared. When we reached Périgueux I detached myself from the group for a day and, borrowing one of the Jeeps assigned to it, drove over to St Martin.

I was apprehensive about what I would find. For all I knew there might have been fighting there and so much could have changed in the six years I had been away. If Marie had been betrayed by someone from the village, maybe there would be hostility to be met. I was also concerned about what I would find at La Garenne. I quite expected it to have been ransacked, if it was even still standing. When I reached the brickworks at the top of the hill everything seemed normal though. There seemed to be work going on and the garage looked as though it was still active.

I turned off and threaded my way slowly down to the village. Two houses on the outskirts had been burned out, but the centre of the village looked to be as it always was except for some German slogans that had been partially obliterated with red paint. I stopped the car and sat there just taking it all in. I was terrified, both at how people would react to me and what I would hear about Marie if anyone was prepared to talk about her and who had betrayed her. However there was nobody around and, rather than go knocking on doors to find someone able to help, I decided in the end to take the back road and go on to La Garenne.

As I drove up the lane it looked as if no-one had been along there for some time. The grass was long even in the wheel-tracks and there were branches hanging down which would have been broken by a vehicle passing by. In the open Jeep I had to duck as I drove along and in doing so I felt my spirits rise. If no-one had been there, maybe the house and all my possessions would be all right.

My hopes remained high as I drove into the courtyard. The back door was shut and there were no signs that anyone had broken in. I climbed out of the Jeep and felt for the key which I had hidden behind one of the window lintels. I shivered when I found that it was not there. My optimism dashed, I went and found it in the door which I discovered was not locked. I opened it with great misgivings assuming that I would find something terrible inside.

What I saw was not exactly terrible, but came as a great shock. Sitting at the table in the old kitchen was a dishevelled man, unshaven and with unkempt hair. He was asleep, his chin slumped on his chest. He was snoring and seemed to be dreaming because his arm was twitching as if he was fighting someone or something off. He was very dirty and his clothes were soiled. I found him alarming and drew the gun with which I had been issued before we left England. It was nothing like the little revolver Fizzy's father had given me back in 1914. This was a menacing, heavy Browning, the sort of pistol I had used on the range at Beaulieu and which I hated because it was so powerful. I hoped I would not have to use it, but the man frightened me and I knew that if he tried to attack me I would have to do so.

As I stared at the him the door swung slowly shut behind me and the click of the lock woke him. He opened his eyes and sat up with a start. I pointed the pistol at him and asked him in French what he thought he was doing in my house. He did not answer immediately but just continued to stare at me, his eyes wide open and his bottom lip quivering. When he spoke he did so very quietly in English and with an audible catch in his voice.

"Maman?- It's me, Maman. It's me - Charles."

Then he put his head in hands and burst into tears.

I don't remember what happened then, but I suppose must have fainted, because the next thing I knew I was lying on the floor. I opened my eyes to find Charles bending over me fanning my face with a towel. My head was spinning and there was an acrid smell in my nostrils. I sat up with a start and asked him what had happened. Before he could say anything I realised that what I could smell was cordite and realised that somehow I had fired my gun. I looked at the pistol in my hand and sniffed the barrel. It had indeed been used. Alarmed I looked to see what I had shot and it was only when Charles laughed that I relaxed enough to ask him what had happened.

"You fired it as you fell to the ground "

He pointed at the fireplace.

"Look. There, just below the mantelpiece. You can see where the bullet struck."

Sure enough there was a gash in the stone where the bullet had struck and I could just see the dull gleam of lead at its edge. Where it ended up I could not tell. The shock of knowing that I had fired a shot momentarily distracted me from my son who coughed to attract my attention. This brought me back to my senses.

It was one of the most joyous moments of my life to be reunited with Charles. I had feared him dead when the Germans overwhelmed the British before Dunkirk. And later I feared him harmed or damaged by life in a prison camp. But he seemed to have emerged reasonably unscathed. We sat for a long time at the kitchen table while he told me all that had happened to him since he had left the POW camp in eastern Germany where he had spent the war. It seems that the Germans had simply abandoned the place one day and he and his fellow inmates had been free to walk out and to find their own ways home. He had chosen not to stay with a group and had headed for the French border which he established was over 200 miles away. By dint of walking, hitching lifts and finally stealing a motorcycle, which gave up the ghost not far from St Martin, he had made it to La Garenne just the night before after being on the road for a long time. He had not known what he would find at the house and the last thing he expected was for me to walk through the door and point a pistol at him.

It was clear that he was as delighted as I was to be reunited. While we talked I was conscious that I would at some point have to break the news to him about Marie. When I did so it added a tragic dimension to our reunion and we were both consumed with our own sad thoughts for a while. I had forgotten how strong the bond between my twins was. When I told him that I believed her to have been betrayed by someone he and his sister must have known in the village his grief turned to anger. He vowed to me that he would seek out and kill whoever it was who had done that to Marie if his identity ever became known. I forbore to say to him that I had already made a vow that if I could find out who it was I would seek him out myself and take my own revenge .

I took him back to Périgueux with me and then on to Bordeaux, where there was a British Army unit that could arrange for his repatriation to London. I returned home a few days later and at the earliest opportunity went to see Vera Atkins. I asked her whether she had been able to shed any more light on Marie's betrayal. At first she was her usual austere self and I began to wonder whether she would be able or willing to help me. Then her manner softened and she talked at some length about the fate of so many of what she called ' her girls'. I realised that my daughter was one of a number of brave young women who had met their deaths in the service of SOE and their country. Vera told me that she had initiated enquiries about Marie's death, but in the postwar chaos in France it might take some time before the truth emerged. Indeed, she added, it might never do so.

I left her angry that no-one could tell me more about how my daughter came to die and more determined than ever that, come what may, I would establish the truth and have my revenge. I do not think Vera was left in any doubt as to my determination to do this and I was comforted by the sense I had that she not only understood my feelings but was willing to do what she could to help me. She did not say as much – that would not have been her style at all - but I could tell that she shared my anger at the death of Marie as well as all those other young women, many of whom had also been betrayed, sometimes by people who were assumed to be trusted colleagues.

At about this time I learned that SOE was to be disbanded and those of its activities that would be appropriate to peacetime were to be merged with MI6. I was offered the chance to join the training staff there but I felt that if I was ever to track down Marie's betrayer I would need to be a free agent and not subject to all the regulations and secrecy of an intelligence service. I therefore declined the offer.

I moved temporarily into Fizzy's house as her Ashley Gardens flat had been damaged by a flying bomb. She was still in Washington and she was only too happy to have someone there looking after her things. Charles lived with me. He seemed fine on the surface but underneath I could detect the damage that all those years of incarceration had inflicted. He was one of many whose lives had been changed if not destroyed by years in a POW camp. He had never been an outgoing boy and now he was shyer than ever, rather reclusive and unable to sleep well. I made it my priority to help him find his feet again. He was lucky that as an officer he had not been made to do manual work for his captors and that with the aid of the Red Cross he had been able to continue his accountancy and banking studies. Now, completely bilingual, he managed to find a job with the London office of the French Banque Nationale. It was a huge relief to have him settled..

Fizzy came back from Washington full of the 'wonderful' war she had had there. She arrived in the Mews in her usual cloud of dust and a huge roar in a vast supercharged car that she had shipped home. I was so pleased to see her again that I rather went to pieces when she arrived. I desperately needed a friend on whose shoulder to lean and, ever the best and only real friend I had ever had other than Jean-Paul and Archie, she was only too willing to be just that. I realised then how lonely I had been since she had left for Washington. Telling me that I was not to be a 'Silly Goose' – which was what she always called me when I was upset - Fizzy was clearly pleased to see me too and she also became quite emotional and said how much she still loved me and how she had missed me. We drank too much that first night and and we both became rather sentimental as the evening wore on.

It was so good to have my old friend back with me. I realised then that for a long time I had needed someone who knew me well to whom I could talk and I poured my heart out to her. As the days passed and with her patient help I was able to start thinking about my own future. I did not need to find a job – what I earned from the flats the Duke had left me and the houses I had bought with my father's money brought in much more than I needed and I also had left behind a large sum of money in France from the sale of the business which I hoped would still be there if my bank had been able to conserve its assets during the occupation. What I wanted was something that would fulfil me and at the same time leave me free to find out the truth about Marie's death. Fizzy, as always, came up with the best idea. She suggested that I simply go back to France, put La Garenne back into its pre-war state and then begin to breed and train horses again. She said that I could put to real use the tricks I had learned from my father. She was in no doubt that I would become famous for my 'talking' skills. My pursuit of Marie's betrayer could be conducted in parallel.

My first reaction was to reject her advice. I loved horses and had lived with them since I was a child, but I did not think I could or would want to make them my life. I was also shy of advertising my ability to calm horses down, sensing that people thought it was a sort of trickery. But the more we talked and the more I thought about it the more I realised that Fizzy was correct. Charles would be all right now that he had a job, Fizzy would be a frequent visitor and I would be better able to find the man in France than from London. Looking after horses meanwhile would be the perfect thing for me to do.

So, early in 1946 I packed up the few things I had accumulated during the war and sent them ahead by rail. Then Fizzy drove me to St Martin in her monster car. We reached La Garenne in the late afternoon of the third day of our journey after stops in Paris and Tours. It was cold and bright and there was a thin covering of snow on the lane as we drove under the bare walnut trees that flanked it. In the last yards the house suddenly came into view. I can recall even now the feeling of immense joy tinged with sadness that overwhelmed me as Fizzy stopped the car. For a while I could only sit there and gaze at the old stone buildings and wonder what the future would hold for me.

Fizzy was a marvel. Without her I would not have known where to start. She stayed for two weeks and by the time she left my luggage had arrived and been unpacked. I had called in builders to discuss improvements to the house and to plan for the building of stables, fencing of the fields and the creating of a schooling ring . More importantly I reconnected with Jean-Paul's family and the friends I had had before the war. The prospect of life at La Garenne no longer daunted me as much as it had when the idea was first mooted.

The only thing that I could not address properly was Marie's death. People in the village always veered away from the subject whenever it looked as though it might become a matter of discussion. Slowly, though, I learned of the harm done to the village during the war by the Germans and their collaborators and began to piece together exactly what had happened to her.

What amazed me initially was the discovery that those who collaborated with the Nazis were far more ferocious in their persecution of anyone who resisted the occupation than their Gestapo masters. There were horrendous stories of whole families being arrested for expressing anti-German sentiments in the earshot of a member of the Milice, the French 'guardians' of the so-called 'Free' sector of France. Formed in 1943 and staffed by zealots, rabid anti-semites and a large body of what I can only call the criminal riff-raff, the Milice committed some outrageous crimes and in post-war France they were widely hated and whenever possible arrested and made to stand trial for their crimes. I learned that one of the houses on the outskirts of the village that had been burned to the ground had been set alight with its occupants inside because someone had alleged, incorrectly as it turned out, that it was a Resistance safe house. Another atrocity had been the entrapment in a cave above the river not far from La Garenne of a number of young men who had beaten up one of the Milice men who had ordered the burning of the house. Herded into the cave, all eight of them had been killed, some blown to bits when a grenade was thrown at them, others smashed to pieces on the rocks below the cave when they jumped down into the river in a bid to escape the blast.

Once I knew of this I felt able to begin asking people whom I trusted and who might know about Marie's death to tell me what they knew. At first no-one appeared willing or able to say anything. Then one evening a small group of villagers accompanied by the Mayor and the Priest came to the house and said they wanted to tell me what had happened to her. Apparently she had been betrayed by a man called Jacques Maziere who had been born in St Martin, was at elementary school with the twins and, by a bitter irony, had worked for me as a mechanic when I had the garage. I recalled him quite clearly. The villagers told me that he had joined the Milice when it was formed and had risen quickly in its ranks. As a result he had good links to the Gestapo. I knew from Vera Atkins, that Marie had been spotted getting off a train at Angoulême and learned that it was Maziere who had been there on the same evening and had recognised her. He had not hesitated to turn her in. Worse, it had been he who had proposed that she should be brought back to St Martin to be executed as a warning to anyone who lived there who had any thoughts of helping the Allies. The Germans approved the idea and Maziere was ordered to arrange things.

My informants hesitated at this point and the Priest asked me whether I wished to have the full story. I dreaded hearing how my beloved daughter had been killed but I had to know all the facts if I was to carry out my vow to avenge her death. I therefore said that I wanted them to continue and in hushed tones they told me that after Marie had been brought to the village the whole population had been forced to come to the square outside the Mairie to listen as the charges against her were read out by Maziere. Then she had been tied to a tree beside the church and a firing squad made up of his men. On a command from him they had fired and she died in a hail of bullets. Her body was taken away and no-one knew where she had been buried, if, indeed, they had bothered to dignify her death with a burial. I remember so well sitting down at my kitchen table after hearing this and staring blankly at the fireplace unable even to cry. The Mayor tried to console me but, realising that I needed to be alone with my grief, he and the group slipped quietly away.

Armed with the knowledge of who had betrayed my daughter I spent the next few days plotting my revenge. I remembered Maziere as a podgy, spotty youth who had been a good enough mechanic at the garage, but not someone I particularly liked. I had only employed him because I felt sorry for him. He was an only child who had been born in 1919 a few weeks after his father had died from wounds inflicted at Verdun at the end of the first World War. His mother had struggled to bring him up and the village had helped her in whatever way they could. My contribution came when Marie brought him home and asked if I could find him a job. He had been willing enough to learn and I had no complaints on that score. What I did not like, though, was the way he pestered Marie, on whom he obviously had a crush. Marie repeatedly told him that she was not interested in his overtures but to no avail. I know that when we left France she was relieved to be rid of him. That he should have been the author of her death suggested to me that he had taken his revenge in a cruel and vindictive way and I wrote immediately to Vera Atkins telling her what I had learned and asking if she had any traces of him.

I heard nothing from her for some weeks and then a brief letter arrived apologising for her tardiness and thanking me for the information. She had a very few traces of Maziere in her records but had no idea whether he had survived the last days of the war and, if so, what had happened to him or where he now was. She promised to do her best to find out and to let me know. I felt crushed by this. I had hoped either to hear that he had been caught, tried and executed when peace came or that his whereabouts were known and that he could be apprehended and brought to justice.

The works at La Garenne were finished by the early summer and the place was transformed. Not only did I have everything I needed for the horses but the house now had better plumbing and wiring and had been turned into a rather grand country house. Had I wished I suppose I could have showed off and called the property a 'domaine', classing it with the other grand houses thereabouts. I resisted that temptation, though, as I thought it ostentatious and felt that my French neighbours would have disliked it.

By the end of the year I had bought some horses to train and had my first problem stallion whose owner, a local landowner called André Dafoe, had asked me to cure it of the habit of bolting when it heard gunfire. My instinct, I confess, was to tell the man not to ride anywhere near a shoot, but I bit back the words and accepted the challenge promising that I would cure the poor animal if I could have him for six months. So Pegasus came to live at La Garenne

I was terrified that my confidence in my self-proclaimed skills might be greater than my abilities and for the first few weeks I was convinced that I was going to fail. Then I discovered quite by chance that what really scared the horse was not the sound of guns but his master's own reaction to them. I found this out because one Monday morning, unbeknownst to me, the local hunt were out looking for a wild boar that had been shot and wounded the previous day. In the fading light they had not been able to find it to give it the *coup de grâce*. When it was light enough the next morning to continue the search they had found the poor beast in the woods at the edge of my large paddock and duly finished it off. I happened to be out there at the time 'talking' to a newly arrived mare which had developed a nasty habit of biting people. The shots fired by the hunters were loud and close, but Pegasus took not a blind bit of notice of them and just went on grazing as if nothing had happened.

I recalled that once my father had been faced with a similar problem and it turned out that the horse disliked the fact that its owner sweated a great deal when out riding. With anyone else it was as calm and well-behaved as could be hoped for, but, when the owner mounted , its sole aim seemed to be to throw him off. The solution was to persuade the owner to sell the horse and buy another. In this case I opined that it was the owner who hated the sound of guns and his unease was transmitted to the horse who then reacted adversely.

I went to see M. Dafoe and put it to him quite bluntly. At first he had blustered and dismissed the idea as fanciful, but eventually he did admit that he did not like the sound of gunfire as it reminded him of his experiences at the front in the 1914-18 war. I asked him if the sound of gunshots made him break out in a sweat. He thought for a while and then admitted that he supposed it did. I explained my theory and told him about the shooting of the boar and the fact that Pegasus was completely unmoved by the sound. I told him that his only solution was to find another horse. Indeed I went as far as to suggest that he give me his horse and that I would give him one of mine. To my surprise and great pleasure he not only agreed but promised that he would tell his friends about my way with horses. That, I suppose, was the beginning of what proved to be a rewarding and successful business.

In the spring of 1948, out of the blue, Fizzy announced that she would like to come to live permanently in France and, if I did not object, she would live with me. I did not know what to say. On the one hand I did not want anyone interrupting the pattern of my life. On the other, I was alone much of the time and was sometimes lonely. And Fizzy was such an old and dear friend. So I agreed and left it to her to decide when and how to come.

Having done that I was determined not to let her presence at La Garenne intrude too much into my life. So I called in the village builder and commissioned him to turn the old dairy beside the barn where I kept Boanerges into a self-contained suite for her. There would be a bedroom, a bathroom, a kitchen and a nice sitting room. She could therefore be independent of me if she wished and, by the same token, I would be able to get away from her when I wanted to be alone. When the job was done I was very pleased: it looked really nice and this spurred me to make some more alterations in the main house too. The kitchen was very old fashioned and the lighting there, though I had had some work done on it when I returned after the war, was not very good. I was pleased with the results.

Fizzy duly arrived one summer evening in yet another grand car - this time it was an Allard, a great red monster with a long bonnet and a cockpit like an aeroplane's. I was always interested in what she was driving but I confess I had lost any desire to own something like that myself. I had kept the old Rolls going and used it from time to time, as much to ensure that it was still running well as for any practical purpose. I had a tractor for use on the farm and a Jeep that I had bought at a sale of old wartime vehicles in Bordeaux for running around the village. I also bought an Army lorry that I converted into a horsebox. Lastly I had a *traction avant* Citroën that I used if I wanted to go any distance. The mechanical skills I had learned from my father meant that I could keep all these vehicles in reasonable order. Indeed, I rather enjoyed tinkering with them. In a way they were like the horses: they worked well for most of the time as long as I 'fed and watered' them but just occasionally I had a problem that challenged me.

As for the horses, there was a steady stream of them, each with their own problem and I loved the challenge of putting them right. Often it was as simple as it had been with Pegasus, but sometimes there were deep roots to the issues I was faced with. The hardest were the animals that had been ill-treated, especially the donkeys, which had usually been overworked and beaten. They were confused and wary when they arrived and very hard to connect with. I had been intending to carry on breeding horses too, but realised that would hinder the work I was able to do for the troubled animals that came my way in increasing numbers.

Fizzy loved what she immediately called her 'new apartment' and soon settled in. I quite thought she would only stay a while and then, restless as ever, would head off somewhere else. But to my amazement and, I have to admit, deep gratification, she stayed for years. She stayed, in fact, until she died.

Not long after Fizzy came to live at La Garenne two things happened that were going to profoundly affect me. The first concerned Charles, who announced that he was being sent to India by his bank. With independence there was concern in the Paris headquarters that its branch in the French enclave of Pondicherry would become isolated unless it had on its staff people who could maintain good relations with the Indian as opposed to the British Colonial administration. Because he was as English as he was

French he was deemed to be the right sort of person to be posted there. He came down to St Martin to break the news and I confess I found it hard to know what to say. He was keen to go. It offered a chance to do something new in a new world far away from the rigours of post-war England. He told me that he also felt that he could escape some of the memories of imprisonment that continued to haunt him. For my part, I feared that he might go and never come back, which would mean that I would have lost both my children. Fizzy persuaded me that I should not stand in his way any more than I would have wanted my parents to have done so to me. This was an argument that never failed to floor me as I knew she was right. That the last time she used it led to Marie's death should not, I knew, make me stop Charles from doing what he wanted, so in the end I consented. Not, I imagine, that my consent or otherwise would have made any difference: he was as determined to go as was Marie. His visit was brief and we had an emotional farewell. I remember waving him off when the taxi came to take him to the station and thinking that it might be the last time I would see him. Fizzy, as always, told me not to be a silly goose, but I think she really understood what I felt.

The second thing was a letter from Vera Atkins in which she told me that she had good reason to believe that Jacques Maziere was living under an assumed name in Poitiers where he ran a garage and a taxi company not far from the station. He was known now as Jean Martin and Vera's informant had told her that he had a protector somewhere high up in the Ministry of the Interior, someone who, like him, had been involved with Milice matters during the occupation. She gave an address and promised to let me know as and when she learned more. She did not say what, if anything, she wanted me to do with this information but I imagined that she was aware that I might wish to to follow it up. So I did not bother to clear things with her. I just wrote to say thank you and left it at that.

Fizzy and I debated for a long time what we could actually do about Maziere and agreed eventually that someone should go to Poitiers to take a look at the garage and to see if it was possible to confirm that it was indeed him. The training I had received at Wanborough had taught me the rudiments of what they used to call operational security and I knew that it would be unwise to do anything that might alert him to my interest in him. So in the end it was Fizzy who drove up there by herself, using the Citroen rather than her flashy roadster, to take a preliminary look. She came back having managed to take some photos of the place and of a group of people on the forecourt of the garage which, when I had them developed, confirmed that one of them was indeed the man who had betrayed and killed Marie.

What to do next posed a problem. I was determined that I would have my revenge even if it cost me my freedom or, at worst, my life, but what I wanted to do was to achieve my objective in such a way that allowed scope to expose Maziere for what he was after he was dead. The plan in my head was that once I had executed him - that was how I saw it: a death penalty for a murder - I would somehow be able anonymously to alert the press as to his true identity and let the story run from there. I was cautious because I was aware that I was way out of my depth, but so strong was my desire for vengeance that I did not really care if I was caught. Once more it was Fizzy who cautioned me to be sensible about this. What was the point, she argued, in risking my life when it should be possible to achieve my objective without doing so.

I confess I went to pieces a bit. The long years of waiting to learn whether revenge would ever be mine were over and now I found that I could not even begin to work out how I could carry out my plan. Fizzy persuaded me that I should be patient, take a look at the garage for myself and then try to work out whether there was a way we could monitor the pattern of Maziere's day and work out where he went, where he lived and so forth. Once we had done that, she argued, we could then decide what we could possibly do.

So Fizzy drove me up to Poitiers to see for myself. We used the Citroen again and decided to stay overnight. This turned out to be the best possible thing in the end. In the day time there was no chance to do more than drive past a couple of times to see what the garage was like and whether we could spot Maziere. The first time he was nowhere to be seen and the taxi that Fizzy had observed was gone. I wondered whether that meant that he was its driver. When we returned in the early evening the taxi was back and there he was standing in the forecourt chatting to another man. I ducked down just in case he spotted me but was able to see enough to confirm that it was indeed him. Fizzy said that he paid no attention to us, which was reassuring. We made another drive past much later. The garage was closed by then but there were lights on in the little flat above the workshop and we could see someone moving about. It occurred to us that it was probable he lived above the shop.

We went back to our hotel outside the city speculating on what we should do next. Fizzy, normally all for doing things on the spur of the moment, was uncharacteristically cautious. She said that she thought we should go home the next morning and plan the next move carefully. There was, she said, no rush and it was better to succeed than to fail because of a lack of planning. Revenge, she reminded me, was a dish best eaten cold. I knew she was right and did not argue. I sat silently in the car with my head spinning while she drove us home.

Back at La Garenne I left Fizzy at the house and walked down to the river, my head still full of ideas and fears. When I reached the point on the bank opposite the cave where Maziere and his Milice had killed those young people, I stood gazing up at the rock-face and let everything fall into place. I had found the man who killed my daughter, I would return and I would kill him. I know this sounds bloodthirsty, but as far as I was concerned this was unfinished war business and I had every intention of completing the job. Once I had decided what I wanted to do and how I would do it my resolve had hardened. I went back to the house with a plan all worked out in my mind.

Fizzy was in her 'apartment' so I went and sat with her. She listened patiently as I told her what I had decided. I told her that all I wanted was to do to him what he did to others, including Marie. I would show him no mercy. I just wanted him dead. My plan was to go back to Poitiers, go to the garage late in the evening, rouse him, confront him and then dispose of him. I would then simply leave and let matters take their course. Someone would find his dead body the next day and that would be that. Fizzy protested that I might be seen, that someone would hear the gunshot or that I would leave finger prints. They would be bound to trace me. She became quite agitated.

I calmed her down and explained that there would be no gunshots, though I would take my little revolver with me just in case. I had learned in my SOE days that the most effective way to kill a man silently was to apply pressure to the carotid arteries in the neck until the blood flow stopped. This would cause the heart to stop too and to anyone other than a specially trained pathologist it would appear that he had had a heart attack. Foul play would not be suspected.

Fizzy took some convincing, but in the end she accepted that I was right and that if I was careful and made sure that I was not spotted entering and leaving the garage no-one would be able to trace me. Indeed, I would ensure that in any case I was sufficiently well-disguised going to and from the place to be unidentifiable. I told her all this with great confidence, though I confess I was alert to the possibility that something could go wrong. I did not show this to her. It was vital that she remained calm and did as she was asked and nothing more.

I told her that I wanted her to drive me to Poitiers again and we would book into a different hotel, one not far from the station and where Maziere lived. I would leave her there and go off to reconnoitre the area and then return to bide my time. I would wait until I was sure that the garage had closed and the flat was occupied. Then I would go and knock on the door and, assuming that it was Maziere who came to the door, I would make him let me in by whatever means were required. Inside I would produce my gun, tell him who I was if he failed to recognise me and make him sit in a chair. I would bind him with a thin rope that I would have in my pocket and then I would kill him as planned. Once he was dead I would remove the rope, let myself out and go to find her in the hotel. We would then leave early in the morning just like normal travellers and drive home. She kept pointing out all the pitfalls in my plan but I ignored her. My only objective was to kill Maziere and to be honest I did not care if in the process I was caught or killed myself. I did not tell Fizzy this, of course.

We drove back to Poitiers a few days later largely in silence. I was acutely aware of the enormity of what I intended to do and I think Fizzy understood this and, sharing my anxieties, left me to my thoughts most of the time. In my bag on my knees was the little pearl handled revolver and I imagined I could feel its weight as we travelled north. At the hotel Fizzy wanted to run over my plan with me, but I did not want to tie myself to something that I could not necessarily keep to. We went out and drove past the garage again mainly so that I could familiarise myself with the layout and then we spent the rest of the afternoon doing touristy things, wandering around the old town centre.

When it was dark I left Fizzy at the hotel and strolled to the station and then on to Maziere's street, calculating as I did so how long it would take me to get back to the sanctuary of our room. It was a good ten minute walk through streets lined with shops that were by then largely closed and houses with name plates on the door that were obviously offices not residences. They too looked blank and unoccupied. I found this reassuring. The fewer people who might be around to see me the better. I paused to put on a head scarf as a sort of disguise then walked on.

When I reached my destination I stood in a doorway across the road from the garage and took stock of the situation. It was closed, the taxi was there, the lights were on upstairs and there was definitely someone moving about. There was no-one to be seen in the street and no passing traffic. The only sound was the clanking of couplings from the marshalling yard nearby and the odd hoot and hiss of steam from a shunting engine. I crossed over, put on a pair of gloves so as to leave no finger-prints while I was inside his flat, took the pistol from my bag and knocked loudly on the door. It took a while before I heard his feet on the stairs and I was alarmed that someone might pass and notice me, but my fears proved groundless. Not a soul was about.

The door was snatched open angrily and without looking closely at me he demanded gruffly what the hell I wanted.

I said very quietly "Good evening Monsieur Maziere."

He looked startled and stared at me.

Then he shouted "My name is Martin not Maziere" and went to shut the door. I put out my foot to stop him and thrust the gun under his nose.

"If you move I shall pull the trigger."

He backed off and I pushed my way into the narrow hallway. Then he recognised me, turned pale and whispered something about having only been doing his duty. Taking my cue from that I told him that I too was only doing my duty - my duty by my daughter. And I indicated with the gun that he should climb back up the stairs.

I was ready for him to try to do something to escape so I kept far enough away to prevent him lashing out at with his arms or legs. I was ready to shoot if I had to. When we reached the top I saw that there was really only one big room there, so I indicated that he should go to the table at one end and sit down. This he did.

Then he demanded in to know what I wanted, repeating that he had had no option over the killing of Marie. I told him that he was a cowardly traitor, that I knew that it was he who betrayed her in the first place and he who had ordered and participated in her death.

'Jacques Maziere' I intoned in what I hoped was a firm enough voice, though I confess I was trembling with fear "I am going to avenge my daughter's death by killing you."

He said nothing, but he looked uncomfortable and I could hear a strange noise. Glancing down I could see water on the floor and realised that he was urinating in his trousers from fear. I remember thinking that he must be a coward as I took the rope from my pocket. I had tied a slip knot with a loop at one end and I put this over his head and down over his arms then pulled it tight. As I did so I warned him that if he moved I would shoot. The blood had drained from his face and he simply stared at me. Then he slumped sideways: he had fainted.

I said once again, in case he was still able to hear, that he was a cowardly traitor, a man who had betrayed his friends, his neighbours in St Martin and his country. As I did so I wound the rope tightly around him to ensure that he could not move his arms. Then taking the risk that he might regain consciousness and try to take evasive action, I put the gun in my pocket and pressed on the sides of his neck as the SOE instructors had shown me at Beaulieu. His head soon fell limply to one side. I cannot recall exactly how long it was before I was satisfied that I had killed him: probably not more than a minute or two but it seemed much longer. I untied the rope, felt for a pulse and found none and then pushed him to see what would happen. He simply fell off the chair and lay unmoving in the pool of his own urine.

I do not remember exactly what I felt. It was partly relief knowing that I had avenged Marie's death. It was partly revulsion though. I was aware that I had done a terrible thing. When I killed Fizzy's attacker all those years before I remember feeling exultation as well as horror. This time there was no joy, just the sickening realisation that I had done something bad, however necessary I deemed it to be.

I put the rope back in my pocket, left the light on in the room but turned off the one on the stairs and made my way cautiously back to the outside door. I opened it very slowly and soundlessly, peering out when I could to see if there was anyone about. At the far end under a street-lamp I caught sight of a dog sniffing the base of a lamp-post, but otherwise there was not a soul in sight. I slipped out of the door closing it quietly behind me and, keeping to the shadowy side of the street, made my way back towards the station taking off the headscarf as I walked. Once I joined the bigger, better-lit streets there were still people about and I made a point of stopping and looking into shop windows as if I was simply taking an evening stroll. To give that some credence I bought a flask of brandy and some savoury biscuits at a small grocer's shop that was still open and bore these back to the hotel. The clerk behind the desk barely raised his head as I crossed the hall to the stairs, murmuring 'Bonsoir Madame' without really looking at me. Then he returned to the newspaper he was perusing without another glance.

Back in the room Fizzy stood up to greet me but said nothing. The tension was too much and I can remember even now the relief I felt as I threw myself on the bed and buried my face in the pillows. Fizzy lay beside me and put an arm round me. She said nothing and we just stayed there in silence for a long while. Eventually I slept and, when I woke, Fizzy opened the Cognac I had bought and poured me some. I drank it gratefully, even though it burned my throat and made my eyes water. It was just the sort of shock to the system I needed and it woke me up. I realised that I was starving having been unable to face eating anything at lunchtime. We went out to see if there was anywhere still open where we could eat. We found a small bistro near the station where we ordered onion soup and a steak. Fizzy still did not ask me about my encounter with Maziere and I found it impossible to even begin to talk about it until we were driving home the next day. Then I told her all and felt much better for being able to do so.

When we arrived back at La Garenne Fizzy took charge. I was still in a state of shock both because I had killed the man and because the emotional impact of having avenged Marie's death had exhausted me. I took to my bed and slept and slept, refusing food and drink for nearly forty-eight hours. I did not say anything, but I also harboured a fear that someone might have noticed me going into or coming out of his home and that the police would arrive and arrest me for murder. Then, as the days passed and nothing happened, I relaxed enough to start tending to the horses in my care and to managing my own affairs again.

The Mayor came to see me a week after our trip bearing a copy of 'Le Monde' in which there was a small item that stated that a man found dead above his garage in Poitiers was a wanted collaborator who had settled there after the war. Although known as Jacques Martin he had been identified from papers in his flat as Jean Maziere and this was confirmed by the police when he was recognised as a Milice commander from the Dordogne whose picture was on a 'wanted' notice. The article went on to say that the man appeared to have died from natural causes - probably a heart attack. The relief I felt was enormous, though I dared not show it to the Mayor.

I bought a copy of the paper and sent it to Vera Atkins with a short covering letter in which I said no more than that I was glad to see that Marie's killer was dead. She sent a rather enigmatic note in reply in which she said 'Well done Diana - Justice has been done.' I took it from what she wrote that she had somehow worked out for herself what had happened. I never met her again. There were numerous invitations over the years to SOE reunions of one sort or another where I would doubtless have seen her, but I wanted no part. I sent some money when they set up the Special Forces Club in London. I never went there though, not least because one letter about the place informed me that photographs of those members of SOE who had lost their lives in the service of their country would be hung on the walls of the main staircase of the building. I had no wish to see my beloved daughter's picture staring out at me when I visited. It would have been a too cruel a reminder of her fate and my loss.

Some months after Maziere's death I decided that there should be memorials for Marie and for all the other people from the village who had been killed by the Germans or the Milice. I went to see the Mayor and said that I would be happy to meet the costs and we agreed that there should be three of them, simple plaques that recorded the names those who had lost their lives at the places where they died. A stonemason was commissioned to submit designs which were accepted and on the anniversary of Marie's death the stones were unveiled with all the village present. One was placed on the site of the house that Maziere had ordered to be burned down with its occupants inside. Another was placed on the rocks beneath the cave where the young people had been killed by the grenade thrown by him. The final one was placed near the church on the spot where Marie had been shot. Each had carved on it a legend that stated that those named had been 'assassinated' by the Germans and their accomplices and each bore the words 'never forget'.

The ceremony for Marie's was very moving and I found it hard to watch the unveiling. There was due to be a *vin d'honneur* after the ceremony, but Fizzy and I went home too upset even to commiserate briefly with the other families. Despite my sorrow, I did feel better though for having marked Marie's role in the fight against the invaders and as the months and then years passed my grief turned into a sort of shrine to the memory of my beloved daughter.

In 1966 when the status of Pondicherry changed and it became a part of India rather than remain an enclave under French control, Charles wrote to say that he would be staying on. He came back briefly the next year for a meeting in Paris and stayed at La Garenne for a few days. He had matured and was a happier man than he used to be. Still somehow resentful at his fate during the war, but fulfilled with his work and clearly happy in India.

A year later he wrote again to say that he had met and fallen in love with a girl who had a French father and an Indian mother. Her name was Angelina. They were to be married very shortly and he apologised that he had not had time to invite me to the wedding. The truth was, he said, that she was pregnant with his child and in order not to add to the prejudice against her for being of mixed race they had decided to wed as soon as possible so that the baby could be born in wedlock. My immediate reaction was a mixture of disappointment not to be there for the wedding and relief that Charles had at last found someone to love. I wrote back immediately, sent some money to help pay for the wedding and said that I would travel out to India as soon as I could to see him and to meet his bride. I was really excited by the prospect and began to make all sort of plans for what would be the trip of my lifetime.

My happiness was short lived though. The wedding was in December 1967 and the baby was born the following May. Charles sent a telegram announcing the birth of Mary Diana Dumont. Then before I had time to respond there was another telegram saying that Angelina had died of complications following the birth. A letter followed that said in effect that he had no option but to stay in Pondicherry for a while so that Angelina's mother could look after the baby. As soon as she was old enough to travel, though, he would arrange to return to Europe so that he could bring up the child in what he called 'his own culture'.

In the summer of 1970 Charles arranged to have himself transferred back to London and I went over there to see him and to meet my grand-daughter for the first time. The three year old Mary was a delight -

pretty, bright and animated. From then on she became my greatest love and I have watched her grow into not only a beautiful and intelligent woman, but also a most talented pianist whose playing has given me and countless others enormous pleasure. She spent many holidays at La Garenne as a child and one day she will inherit the place from Charles. I think she loves it as much as I do. I hope so.

I was so happy to have Charles back in my part of the world again. I like to think that he found contentment bringing up his daughter even though the sadness he felt at the loss of his wife must have been as deep and discomforting as mine was when I lost Jean Paul. He prospered at the bank in London and came out to see me as often as he could. He never really got on with Fizzy. I think he did not understand her. Perhaps I should have told him that neither did I, but somehow I never got around to doing that.

As for Fizzy she did not change over the years. She still drove her fast cars like a lunatic and was always coming up with madcap ideas. She would disappear every so often saying something like 'I'm off to see a friend in New York.' Then weeks later you would get a card from Rio de Janeiro or somewhere else exotic. Then equally unexpectedly she would turn up again and life would go on as if she had never gone away. I did not mind. I like my peace and quiet and being able to be here with my horses, the dogs and the garden was my idea of heaven. As she got older she became more eccentric.

One of her crazy hobbies was sitting in the garden in a deckchair and shooting pigeons with an air-rifle. She was rather good at this and I found myself cooking endless pigeon pies!

I was able to leave the properties in England in the capable hands of Mr Vigus, the agent I found just after the war, who most efficiently dealt with any problems that arose. He was worth every penny of his fee. He also had some useful connections in the world of banking which meant that I could draw on my bank account in London without having to obtain exchange control permission to bring money over here. It was something to do with his brothers, two of whom had links to a small merchant bank in The City and a cousin in Paris who was in a similar position. I think, but do not exactly know, that it was all to do with balancing each other's books without actually physically sending money. High finance was never a world I understood and I was prepared to let Mr Vigus get on with it as long as I did not lose out or run into trouble. I am glad to say that I did not! All I knew was that, if I needed money, a letter to Mr Vigus would result in funds being paid into my bank account in France.

I say the years passed happily and indeed they did. The sadness I felt about Marie never left me, of course, and I did not help myself by making a point of placing flowers on her monument each year. But the wound did heal as the years passed and by the time I reached my 75th birthday I could celebrate with friends at La Garenne and then depart with Fizzy for London the next day to spend time with Charles and Mary.

Fizzy died in 1975. She had once told me that she did not want to live until she was old and decrepit. Jokingly she had once asked me to shoot her if that began to happen. I made it abundantly clear of course that I would do no such thing. She did, in time, become older and slower even though she pretended that nothing had changed. She became a bit absent-minded about dates and times. She also started to reminisce at great length about things we had done in the past, usually prefacing these sessions with the words 'I don't suppose you remember this Dippy' and launching into her story without waiting for me to say whether I did or not. I put up with it because it would have made life more difficult if I stopped her. I think in a funny sort of way she was aware of what she was doing, but that did not silence her. Her health was good enough and passion for fast cars remained, but it seemed to me that for a large part of the time she was not properly in touch with reality.

Her death came as a surprise and a shock. She had announced one day that she was going to drive to Paris to meet up with an old friend from her days in Washington during the war. She set off in her red E-type Jaguar after bidding me her usual fond farewell and telling me that she would spend the night in Tours and be in the capital the next afternoon. I thought nothing of it and carried on with my chores about the farm. But that evening, just as I was about to have my supper, a Gendarme appeared on the doorstep and informed that 'La Comtesse' had been in a car accident and had been taken to the hospital in Tours. I told him I would drive up there immediately to be with her but he advised me that there was no great urgency as she had died shortly after being admitted. He wanted me to go the next day to identify her formally and to make arrangements for her body to be moved to an undertakers before burial.

After he had gone I sat and cried like a baby. The woman to whom I owed so much - almost all my meaningful life when I think about it - was gone and I could not bear the thought. As I drove north the next morning I could not help wondering whether she had killed herself. The last thing she had said to me the day before was 'Never forget, Dippy, you are the person I have loved best in all the world'. At the time I thought it was a bit of Fizzy's gushing, but as I thought about it I came to believe that she was in fact bidding me farewell.

My suspicions were confirmed by the Tours police. They told me that Fizzy's car had left a straight stretch of the road just north of the city and crashed into one of the   large plane trees that lined it. No other car was involved, there were no skid marks and no cause could be established for the accident. The car appeared to be mechanically perfect and the tyres were sound. The weather had been good. It dawned on me that she had indeed committed suicide. It would have been quite in character for her to have decided to kill herself if there was good enough reason to do so.

I drove back to St Martin sad and puzzled. If I was right, I could think of no good reason why she should have taken her own life. If I was wrong, then I wanted to know what had happened. After all, Fizzy was the most significant person in my life. Had I not met her that day in 1914, heaven knows where I would have ended up. Probably at my horrid uncle's after all and I would have married Len Driver, become a war widow and then God knows what would have happened. It did not bear thinking about.

When I reached La Garenne I went to Fizzy's apartment intending to sort out her things and somehow put myself at ease and lay her ghost. But that was not to be. For on the mantle-piece in her sitting room was an envelope addressed to me. I opened it with trepidation fearing what I would find.

The letter was written in her flamboyant script on a large piece of notepaper which bore the Dartmoor crest, just like the letter her father wrote me before he died.

My dearest, darling Dippy.
I am writing this to you to say farewell. It is the saddest and most difficult thing I have ever done. The fact is that I was told by my doctor in London on my last visit home that I only had a few months to live. I have cancer and all sorts of other things wrong with me. He told me, actually, that he could not understand why I had lasted so long! Anyway the upshot is that I have had it. I have no wish to be a burden on you or anyone else and I certainly don't want to just sit and wait for the inevitable.
So, my darling, I am going to kill myself. Don't be alarmed. I shall simply crash my car into a tree and finish things. I know that sounds drastic, but you know me well enough to know that doing things by half is not my style! So this is goodbye, Dippy. I have loved you from the day we met at Adlestrop. My sort of love has never meant anything to you, I know - friendship of course, but the burning physical passion I have always had for you was never reciprocated, I am sad to say. But being able to spend most of my life with you has been compensation enough, though I wish it had been otherwise. It has been a wonderful life and we have done so much together.

I have left you everything I have apart from a few bequests. The house in London and the flats - they're all yours. I think there is a lot of money too - talk to the bankers: they'll know.
All I ask in return is that you will remember me fondly and bury me at Caxton next to my dear Father and Mother.
Goodbye, Dippy my darling. I do love you so much.
Fizzy

I read the letter three or four times and then sat on the bed for a long while wishing she had said it all to me in person. I know she had always felt something for me I could not feel for her, but I never really understood how strong that feeling was. I felt guilty and angry at the same time. How could I have been so stupid not to have known. But, also, how stupid of Fizzy not to tell me. I suppose she thought she had tried and then when I did not react as she hoped I would, she just bottled everything up and decided that it was better to live close to me rather than at a distance and be lonely. The anger disappeared and just the guilt remained, even though I know I could never have loved her in the way she wanted to love me. I felt so sad.

I must have been there for a long while unaware of the passing of the hours because when I heard the telephone ringing I looked up and saw that it was dark outside. I made my way across to the kitchen. It was Charles ringing to see how I was. I am afraid I kept him on the line for a long time pouring out my heart to him about Fizzy. He was so kind and patient and when he eventually rang off I felt much better. He promised to contact Fizzy's solicitor the next morning and left it to me to arrange with a funeral director in France to take the body back to England.

Over the next few days I had so much to do that it was only in the quiet of the night that I had time to mourn. It was slowly dawning on me that Fizzy had meant more to me than I realised. She had of course been a part of my life for ever, but it was only now that I saw that the closeness of our friendship was not unlike that of an old married couple. Before, I suppose, I had somehow taken her for granted. Suddenly I was missing that special ingredient, the companionship of someone who knows you and understands you, not always agreeing with you, but totally supportive and prepared to protect you as and when things go wrong. My grief grew as the days passed.

Charles was a huge help and between him and the most efficient undertaker Fizzy's body was taken home to England and I rushed back to England to be there for the funeral. To my surprise there was quite a crowd at the church made up of friends from London, members of the FANY and a good contingent of people young and old whose forebears had had a connection with her family at Caxton Magna. She was buried next to her father and mother and beside the simple monument to Hex, whose body had never been found on the battlefield at Mons. I felt completely bereft as I saw the coffin lowered into her grave. I have never been one to look back, but that day I felt my life flash by and realised more strongly than ever that Fizzy had been a vital part of it.

Before I left London at his request I called on old Mr Coombs, Fizzy's solicitor, who read me her will. Apart from some bequests, the principal one being to the FANY, I was the sole beneficiary. He was unable to place a final value on her estate but it was clear that I would be considerably richer when the will was proved. I did not need for money, so I asked him to place the capital in trust and to use the income to pay for my granddaughter's education and her musical training. I also made sure that there was enough money to provide Charles with a proper pension when he chose to retire.

I went back to France feeling very low. Fizzy's death had made me aware that the clock was ticking for me too. I was getting on for 80 and, though I felt as fit as a flea, I knew that one day something would happen to change that. I remember wondering how I would cope in the future: but cope I did. I carried on at La Garenne for several more years, gradually reducing the number of horses I cared for and hiring men from the village to look after the garden and grounds. Charles visited regularly and Mary spent every holiday with me. In 1980 Charles was made redundant following a merger of his bank with another and he came out to live permanently with me. This was a great comfort, as I had grown lonely living there by myself.

A year ago I was told by my doctor that I had a form of leukaemia that could only be treated with some drastic chemotherapy. I was given the choice of doing nothing, in which case I would live for a year at least, maybe longer. The treatment might postpone my death but I would find that it would reduce the quality of my life. I would lose my hair, I would become very fat and I would probably feel awful most of the time.

I was nearly 90 so I opted for doing nothing. This is what prompted me to sit down and write this story of my life before it was too late. I have been honest and I have also tried to say everything that I feel should have been said. I hope that when Charles and Mary read it they will understand me better and, perhaps, see something of me in themselves. I have had an amazing life and I regret nothing except the deaths of my beloved husband, my heroic lover, my darling daughter and my much-loved friend.

I ask nothing of those who will have to make the arrangements for my funeral except that that they arrange for my body to be cremated and for some of my ashes to be scattered at Adelstrop station where my adventures began and the rest around Fizzy's grave at Caxton. That is probably not allowed, but I hope a little of my capacity for breaking the rules will have been passed on and that Charles and Mary will throw caution to the winds along with all that remains of me.

That was how the journal ended.

At back of the book I found an envelope containing several photographs. The first was of a young couple who, I assume from their dress, were my great-grandparents. They looked very formal and serious and I wondered whether it had been taken when they became engaged to be married. The second was of a young girl standing by a horse outside a stable: that surely had to be Granny. Then there was one of a handsome , dark-haired man about to climb into a lorry laden with bricks - I assumed that was my Grandfather. The next was of two children in their teens, clearly twins, who I was sure were my father and his sister Marie. Then there was a snap of a dashing young airman in uniform standing by a small biplane and waving at the camera. That had to be Archie. The last was of two middle-aged women standing beside a powerful-looking car. One of them was tall and blonde with a slightly manic grin on her face who I recognised as Fizzy. Granny, shorter and dark-haired, was standing next to her smiling contentedly. I could see that it had been taken at La Garenne. I looked at them in turn thinking how wonderful it was that you could encapsulate a whole life in just a few snapshots. Then I closed the book and sat for a long while quite overwhelmed by what I had just read.

I had no idea if my father had read it too, but as he never mentioned it before he died, I assume he had not. Perhaps he never even knew of its existence. If that was the case it meant that he would not have known about Granny's life nor what she wanted after her cremation.

I had no idea where the ashes might be, but I remembered that the crematorium had sent us a casket in a box which had sat on the kitchen mantelpiece for a long while. I looked for it but it had vanished. I eventually tracked it down in one of the cupboards in the hall. I determined there and then that when I went back to England I would carry out her wishes, even though I had no idea where Adlestrop and Caxton Magna were. The casket was still full so I went through the somewhat macabre process of dividing the ashes into two piles and putting each into a separate plastic bag.

Then, when I returned to London the following week, I worked out where I had to go to scatter them and on a fine day two weeks later drove out to Oxfordshire with the casket on the passenger seat beside me.

At Adlestrop, which proved to be a charming small village with pretty stone houses, some with thatched roofs, I learned that though the station had closed back in the 1960s, the line was still in use. On the little patch of grass near the post office and village shop was a shelter in which hung one of the old station signs. Perhaps it was the very one that Granny had stood behind when she left the train. Also in the shelter was a bench on which printed on a small plaque was the text of Edward Thomas's poem about the train, the poem I had found in the front of Granny's journal.

I sought directions to the railway line and there found what was left of the station, now just a few buildings and a number of vehicles. I parked near the road bridge over the line and walked up to stand directly above the track. I said a little prayer for 'Dippy', as I had begun to call her in my mind, and then emptied out the contents of one of the bags of ashes onto the track below. I stood for a moment longer and thought about the remarkable story that had begun there. It gave me a real thrill to be almost exactly where it had all started. As I gazed down the line and thought about the poem I became aware of a blackbird singing its heart out in the bushes nearby. How fitting, I thought.

As I walked back to the car a train went through at high speed and I took pleasure in the thought that the wind it created in its wake must have scattered Granny's ashes far and wide. Like the birdsong in the poem they were now spread all over Oxfordshire and Gloucestershire!

I found Caxton Magna with difficulty. It turned out, when I enquired, that the old house had burned down years ago when it had been some sort of secret laboratory. It its place was a rather nasty utilitarian building still owned by the Government who had commandeered the property in 1940. The guard on the gate directed me to the little church on the far edge of the estate where I found the tombs of the Dartmoor family. There must have been many of them buried there over the centuries, but the ones I sought were those of the late Duke and Duchess, Viscount Hexworthy and The Lady Fiona Moretonhampstead to give Fizzy her proper title. They were tucked away under a pretty tree at the back of the graveyard, looking neglected. I spent a little time sweeping off the dead leaves with my hands and pulling out some of the tall weeds that had encroached. Then I said another little prayer over Fizzy's stone and scattered the other bag of ashes. I did not just pour them around Fizzy's grave but round the others too because of the part each had played in Dippy's life.

I drove away feeling truly sad to have said farewell to two people whose stories had so enthralled me and to whom I reckoned I owed so much. I envied them their adventures and their loves. I felt sad for Fizzy for her unrequited passion for Dippy. I felt sorry for the gallant Hex who had died so young for his country and for the old Duchess dying of a broken heart after his death. I had a special sadness for the Duke, whose generosity had made Dippy's and therefore my fortune. I just wished that I could honour the grave of Archie in the same way, but his body lay deep under the sea and would have to be honoured just by Dippy's love for him which she recorded with such passion in her journal.

When I got home I was seized with the need to somehow express my thoughts about Granny's story and I wrote the following poem which I like to think somehow sums up that extraordinary day in 1914 when she took her fate in her own hands and started out on her adventures.

Maybe someone did get off the train
that hot June afternoon
and the poet missed the shutting of a door.
He did not see a dark-haired girl
use the brief unscheduled stop
to leave a life she did not want
and slip away to find another world.
Then, as a steam valve hissed
the couplings clanked,
and the train moved on again
he could not have known
she stayed there all alone
listening to a blackbird sing.

The End

Lightning Source UK Ltd.
Milton Keynes UK
UKOW042107171012

200755UK00002B/200/P